VINCENT THE VILE
VAN GOON
First Mate

SLIME BUCKET
SAM
Gunner

SOUTH CENTRAL REGIONAL LIBRARY

Miami Branch
MAY 2010
$2.00

SCREEMIN' MEENA
Navigator

FAMOUS AMOS
Brute

IRONBOUND IKE
Brute

CRANKY FRANKIE
Knotjack

O9-BTJ-641

T·H·U·G·S·S·

··UNION··
CERTIFIED

ZEKE THE GREEK
POPADOPOULOS
Slopjack

WEDGIE REGGIE
Jury-Rigger

MIAMI
Community Library
MIAMI MB R0G 1H0

The Dread Crew

PIRATES OF THE BACKWOODS

KATE INGLIS

ILLUSTRATIONS SYDNEY SMITH

NIMBUS
PUBLISHING LTD

Copyright text © Kate Inglis, 2009
Copyright illustrations © Sydney Smith, 2009

All rights reserved. No part of this book may be reproduced, stored in a
retrieval system or transmitted in any form or by any means without the prior
written permission from the publisher, or, in the case of photocopying or other
reprographic copying, permission from Access Copyright, 1 Yonge Street, Suite
1900, Toronto, Ontario M5E 1E5.

Nimbus Publishing Limited
PO Box 9166
Halifax, NS   B3K 5M8   (902) 455-4286

Printed and bound in Canada

Design: Heather Bryan
Author photo: Kate Inglis

Library and Archives Canada Cataloguing in Publication

Inglis, Kate, 1973-
The dread crew : pirates of the backwoods / Kate Inglis ;
illustrated by Sydney Smith.
ISBN 978-1-55109-737-4

I. Smith, Sydney, 1980- II. Title.
PS8617.N52D74 2009   jC813'.6   C2009-903632-0

Canada Council | Le Conseil des Arts
for the Arts | du Canada

NOVA SCOTIA
Tourism, Culture and Herit

We acknowledge the financial support of the Government of Canada through
the Book Publishing Industry Development Program (BPIDP) and the Canada
Council, and of the Province of Nova Scotia through the Department of Tourism,
Culture and Heritage for our publishing activities.

This book was printed on
Ancient-Forest Friendly paper

ANCIENT FOREST
FRIENDLY™

For my three boys—one is all energy and marvel and curiosity, one is pure, sheer joy and wanderlust, and one lives high up in a blue sky, in a roofless, sheepskin-draped room with kind minstrels and acrobats that let him stay up late and eat chocolate by starlight. All three are hooligans and inventors, and the sons of a man with the steadfastness of a thousand quilters.

Contents

Prologue

Under the darkest cloak of night, her cats are first to sense the rumble.

Alarm ripples through the air and they dart into small spaces, crouching underneath crumpled paper and behind the stove and atop the highest piles, eyes glistening and lit with danger.

She is the colony queen, feral herself, trusted despite her humanity. She snores soundly in her cot through the approach of an engine, the creak of the door, the heft of unwelcome boots. Finally, a hiss penetrates the old woman's ear like an electric prod and she shoots up at the warning of her untame sons and daughters.

"I know it is you," she calls into blackness to her slinky wilderbeasts, the moth-eaten blanket fallen round her waist. "Evening time is for mother's rest, darling rascals. If you must play and hunt then do so outside. Go and find some juicy rats, my lovelies."

A long, low growl says *Danger!* and she stiffens.

"Juicy rats?" The deepest voice she has ever heard hits her

with a sour wind. "Sounds delicious, but if yeh don't mind, ma'am, we's already had our midnight tasties."

A glow through the window illuminates the face belonging to the deepest voice, only inches from her own, and she sees blisters and boils, hair matted and tangled, grime and guck that drips with a pit-pit-pat onto her lap. She registers many figures beyond, some so giant they crane their heads sideways, shoulders and backs pressed to the ceiling.

"Turn it upside down, brutes," the voice snarls, snake eyes unblinking, and the room erupts. The face grins wickedly to a chorus of roars, and behind it a storm of her belongings and her cats recoil through the air with the force of a bomb.

It is the sacking of her shantytown, her warren of patched-together trailers nestled among stacks of rusted rebar and railway ties and forgotten freight. They hiss *Don't you budge an inch, cupcake* as they rifle her things, her most important things, hurling jovial taunts at one another in an almost cheerful way, in the way of satisfying work, a perversion that heaps insult upon injury. She gapes, paralyzed, for she has had this vision, and here it is come to pass. Their funk is thick in her nostrils, and as her stomach churns with fear she finds her lungs and screams, as they always do.

Chapter One

THE TRACKER AND THE PRIZE

The boy was never seen without his backpack, although naturally, no one knew what it was for, because a pirate tracker is only a pirate tracker if that pirate tracker is so in secret.

In it was a flashlight, a topographical county map, bright red sticky dots to mark the evidence trail, plastic bags for sample-collecting, a folding shovel, and a variety of scrapers, chisels, tongs, and tweezers. A tattered journal held together by a web of elastic bands held photographs, sketches, and observations, all recorded with the fastidiousness of a test pilot, or a scientist, or an archeologist, for the boy was a member of that society of explorers who know that record keeping is at the root of discovery.

May 13: the crows were upset today. Treetops at Boutilier's Bog sheared off, disturbing nests.

June 26: mechanical difficulties appear to continue. Found behind the old mill: three (3) large wooden wheel bolts, splintered (see photo); rut left in mud like something got stuck; two (2) empty rolls and wrappers reading SNEERIN' CYRIL'S NO-STOP PINCH-FIX DUCT TAPE (remains catalogued).

He extracted, photographed, and categorized each clue, noting its origin with thumbtacks on the county chart he'd pinned up in the farmhouse attic—for that was his secret station (like a clubhouse without the club, himself being the only pirate tracker he knew of) and it was there he kept evidence stacked in boxes and preserved in specimen bottles. He placed the most precious clues, if size allowed, in an old sailmaker's chest with a false bottom—the litter beyond frayed rope and abandoned bolts that proved the existence of a whole other world and class of life.

Climbing up through the hatch to see the sailmaker's chest sitting there so plainly, he grinned, satisfied. *That's just like me, that old box. Plain on the outside but with more than you'd guess on the inside. With a trick panel that hides the most amazing stuff. That's just like me.*

The story of how Eric Stewart became a pirate tracker is one that begins with boredom, the mother of excitement.

By the measure of farms his was all things interesting— generations old, sprawling and overgrown. Nestled on the edge of a wild wood inland from a meat-grinder sea, there were hurricanes and blizzards and hatches to be battened down. There were long-abandoned forts littered with rusted cannons and piles of grapeshot buried by meadowgrass, and on foggy days the scent of tar and gunpowder lingered in the air. But it was a farm nonetheless, where thrills were as distant a prospect

as distraction, and Eric was without the chatter of brother
or sister to occupy him. Often he would scramble up to an
old watchpost and stare off into the great expanse of forest,
imagining himself tearing along in pursuit of one disturbance
or another. Then he'd sigh, and hop back down, and trudge
across crumbling stone to the shrieks of the peacocks and the
bleating of the goats, to his chores of milking or stirring or
picking.

In just shy of twelve years there had been nothing but woods
and fitful solitude for Eric Stewart. And for the whipsmart
boy with the shock of coarse, white-blond hair, even the most
interesting of ordinary was simply not enough.

"You've got a nose like no one else," his mother had said to him
on that first fateful morning. "It's mulligan stew Monday, and
it's not stew without a little zing, so off with you, love, and don't
you come back till that basket's full."

The sun was still groggy as Eric set off through the fields
and across the creek to the edge of the old woodlot, uncut for
generations now. The once-tamed patch lay on the boundary of
a crown forest so dense it was unwelcoming even to campers,
a corridor of nature at her most riotous. But wily boys are
unbothered by riot, and can venture where trucks and tourists
cannot, and so Eric's boots navigated stray roots and rocks in
a trancelike state as he scanned the overgrowth for sprouts of
stew-bound wild garlic.

His eyes drawn to the sky by ominous rain clouds, he felt a sharp pain to his calf bone and tripped spectacularly, landing in a heap. He righted himself and spun around and as soon as he saw it, this thing that did not belong, a prickly feeling travelled up the back of his neck.

If it hadn't been the size of a barn door and made of wood, he would have guessed it to be a hubcap. Cracked clean through the middle and torn from its cogs, its purpose and fate were plain—this wheel cover had buckled under enormous weight or reckless speed or both. So large it was, though, that if it could ever be hauled upright it would tower far above the head of his father, who had to duck through every doorway. He took several steps back, head cocked to one side, his leg still smarting, and as soon as his eyes and his brain agreed on the sight in front of him he jumped back.

"But that's impossible…"

He shook his head vigorously, blinked, and looked again. The monstrous thing still steamed with heat and smoke, a slime of unknown origin dripping off its tilted end. The only conclusion was unfathomable, but there it was, a mark burned into the centre—the fearsome emblem he knew from storybooks but foreign to these deepest of woods. A charred skull and crossbones.

The mark of pirates.

"My word, boy, that's a nasty bruise on your leg," remarked Eric's mother as she stirred a pot of oats on the wood stove. *Eyes in the back of her head,* thought Eric, fidgeting uncomfortably on his stool. His stomach growled.

"Wasn't watching where I was going…got stuck trying to cross that beaver dam at the marsh the other day, that's all."

"That's not like you." She ruffled his hair, laying a steaming bowl on the table in front of him. "You always watch where you're going. Eat up, now."

Drizzling blackberry syrup over his porridge, he glanced across the table at the headlines of his father's *Daily Clipper* and the blackish-purple stream drifted from the bowl to the table and then onto the floor, his pouring hand wandering absentmindedly, his eyes wide with shock.

HOOLIGANS STRIKE AGAIN: LIMBERGER CHEESE WAREHOUSE LOOTED

WOMEN'S AUXILIARY TEA DISRUPTED BY HOOLIGANS

LUMBERYARD BROKEN INTO AGAIN: HOOLIGANS SUSPECTED

SHANTYTOWN NEAR-DESTROYED IN MIDNIGHT ATTACK

(Splat!) The dripping dishcloth tossed by his mother hit him square in the chest and fell into his lap, bringing him back to his senses. He set the jug back on the table with a clatter and looked up at her.

"Good grief, your head's in the clouds this morning," she huffed. "Sop that up, will you, else we'll all be sticking to the floor for the next two weeks."

"Sorry, Mom." He wiped hastily and stumbled down the back hall from the kitchen, calling over his shoulder. "…Must have…uhhh…slipped."

But he hadn't slipped. He had simply put two and two together.

From then on Eric's eyes were sharpened to the mystery that had always been here, and there, and all over. From between the paws of the Greene's retriever he pulled a discarded foil wrapper that read SIMPERSON'S SUN-DRIED BABY SLUG SNAX endorsed by a "Limpin' Lionel, Tundra Crunch Navigator" *(A boom is a bust with no crunch for your brunch!)*. He discovered broken swaths cut through the forest, the cracks in the bottoms of his boots all stuck up with fresh splinters. From one village to the next he noted reports of disappearing goods, unexplained odours, clusters of jack pines torn up from their roots like matchsticks. Clue after clue pointed to a great disturbance indeed, dropped into his lap as though he'd willed it so out of sheer boredom.

"It's about time someone connected these dots," he said out loud to no one in particular one day as he knelt in the mud, neverminding the stench. "It's meant to be me."

Eric was an inlander, and so was jostled along country roads through Barss Corner to the seaside town of Lunenburg for school. The bus—waiting for it, riding on it—afforded him time to think, and so on this day, like every other one, he walked along the docks to his stop shaking off the residue of note-passing girls and uncooperative fractions. He was consumed, his head down, and registered the approaching figure in the distant, muffled way of an occupied mind. He reared up on her so unexpectedly, he dropped the library stash he'd been carrying (*Orienteering by the Stars*, *The Hawk Tracker's Field Manual*, and *Forensic Methods of Evidence Recovery Volume IV*) and stood there gawking for a moment, the books in disarray at his feet.

"PIRATES!" she cried, a spray of hysterical spittle catching the sun. "THEY HIDE IN THE WOODS, and THEY KNOW WHERE YOU LIVE, and they TAKE WHAT THEY WANT, and VERY ROUGHLY INDEED, and BEWARE!"

The sight of Bertha "Mrs. Knickers" Pringle raving on the docks was hardly uncommon. She was followed by an adoring company of vicious feral cats, as always, and wore all manner of underwear on the outside of her clothes, as always. What got Eric's attention this day was the topic of her rant, her arms sweeping through the air as she moved through a politely indifferent crowd.

"A RIOT, my fellow citizens, a RIOT that SPLATTERS its STINKING SLIME! STINKING and ROLLING as they please and THIEVING, RIPPING, GRABBING..."

Passersby chuckled and shrugged, and some even ventured to pat her on the back dismissively. She shook them off more agitated than ever, careening towards the old dockyard trailing her feline followers and a stream of shrieks.

Eric studied her as she faded into the distance. *There may go a perfectly reasonable source of news.*

The corner of paper was trampled, half-buried but surely not of the forest. Like a paperback novel left in a tent through a thunderstorm, it was curled and swollen with dampness, its pages soaked through. Eric stooped in the mud to investigate, drawn to the wood kiln by the news of a ransacking a few days before. The ink, bled-through and smudged, was just barely legible.

[CLASS 5 CLASSIFIED]
[DO NOT LET LOOSE]
[DO NOT REMOVE FROM CAPTAIN'S QUARTERS]

He stared unblinking at the muck at his feet before turning to pull his spade from the strapping on his pack. He used his foot to press the blade into the earth all the way around, then slid the shovel underneath and pried the handle up. A substantial hunk of mud came free, the paper intact in the middle of it. Into his duffel it went, the whole lot (a good thing, too, that the bag was chocolate brown), and stepping back through the forest he held his prize at arm's length like a live bomb.

He hid the remains to dry, mud and all, in the attic eaves. Thanks to the rising heat of the Stewarts' kitchen wood oven—a hundred-year-old iron hulk in which Eric's dad baked exactly two loaves of rye bread every day—the cube of mud became brittle and dusty, tucked into its own baking compartment in the attic above.

On the eighth day Eric crawled into the eaves. Although he could see very little in the unlit cupboard he smelled a familiar, pungent earthiness, that which did not belong indoors. Suddenly, mere inches from where he knew the block to be, he sneezed violently four times. He backed off, cursing and scrambling for his pocket flashlight. In its glow he saw that the air was filled with a fine brown cloud—all that remained of the dehydrated block of mud, after his disturbing of it—and on the floor of the cupboard was left a modest fold of paper, a fraction of its former self. Eric cradled the artifact in both hands and backed out to the light of the attic window, sitting cross-legged with the pages on the floor in front of him.

It had once been a fat book, its insides torn from the binding as if tangled in some unyielding mechanism. All that remained were a few of the first and a few of the last pages, and the cover.

INTERNATIONAL TREASURE HUNTERS &
USEFUL GOODS SALVAGERS SOCIETY (T.H.U.G.S.S.)
ANNUAL DIRECTORY & ANTIRULES

- RAZEN HANDBOEK -
- MANUEL DE RAGE -
- HANDBOK DU DISKUST -
- MEGAMUK BUK -
- MANUALE INFURIATO -
- HEFTE STORME BOK -
- FURIOSAMENTE MANUAL -
- TUMULTUAR LIVRO -
- INSTRUCCIONES DE LOCO -

[CLASS 5 CLASSIFIED]
[DO NOT LET LOOSE]
[DO NOT REMOVE FROM CAPTAIN'S QUARTERS]
[KEEP LOCKED & GUARDED ONSHIP]

Breathless, Eric turned the pages over. On the back was a partial list of what looked to be a roster and inventory entitled SWORN CONTRACT.

Mick MacKenzie

RIPSAW Mick MacKenzie
CAPTAIN, The Crummies
Hudson Bay Region, Canada
(Fleet of modified bush vehicles [24] led by command unit *Stompin' Tom*; portable camp [1])

Maddock Llewelyn

Maddock SELKIE Llewelyn
CAPTAIN, Meaner Submariners
Bottomless Bay, Orkney Isles
(Typhoon class command unit *Shadow of Stromness*
(a.k.a. *The Shadow*) [1]; two-man scout fleet

ALAISDAIR BLACK

Alaisdair SIR CHUFF Black
CAPTAIN, The Blitzriders
London Underground, England
(Modified four-coupled tank engines of varied vintages
[4: *Kingsgut IV, Sir Eustace, Biggin Hill, Lord Dowdy*];
variety freight cars & sub-engines [est. 15+])

Rasmus Krook

Rasmus HARRIER Krook
CAPTAIN, The Hurks (a.k.a. The Squadroneers)
North American Midwest/Prairies
(Hercules freight aircraft body *Helix* [1] modified w/
helicopter rotors [12]; three-man hot-air scouting shuttles [4])

TERRA JUANITA

Terra THE JAGUAR Juanita
CAPTAIN, The Excavadoras
North Abyssian Jungle, Belize
(Tundra Crunch subterranean command unit *Excavar II* [1];
four-man Devil's Club Dirtpunchers [3])

FRITZI   BRUNHILDA

Fritzi BOHO Faust and Brunhilda THE FIST
CAPTAINS, The Bombadiers
Black Tusk Mountain Range, Desolation Sound
(Mean-Eyed Cat Twin-Hull command units *Ulric* and
Ursidae [2]; snowsled fleet [12])

There were many other signatures where the page had been torn or soaked through, hopelessly illegible and smudged. But what little Eric could make out left nothing to the imagination. The pirate tracker was born.

Chapter Two

THE SKEPTIC'S COMEUPPANCE

"*That* avalanche up on Cypress Mountain, that was somethin' else," the old man spoke aloud to himself as he twisted weeds from mounds of pungent, papery onion. "That chunk of glacier broke off and rolled like a snowball, big as a house. I never ran so fast. That was...what? '82? '84?"

He sunk his head, brow furrowed.

"Those Bella Coola black bears...scrawny fellas. Got 'em away from them loggers, and I swear one of 'em turned around and gave me a wink. Wasn't that just a few springs back? Eight, maybe ten?"

Muttering to himself, he sank again upon the earth.

Sponagle Hollow, a gully of crickets and breeze in poplars and daisy meadows, lay three fields over from the Stewart farm. On this early summer day all appeared as it ever was, serene and unruffled. All except its restless inhabitant. Joe—Grampa Joe, in his latest iteration—was the stuff of legend, his face leathery and weathered from past adventures. When he was young and strong, he'd scaled snow-capped mountains and paddled across the ocean and bushwhacked through the deepest, greenest forests.

These days, one week blurred pleasantly into the next. He was grizzled, rooted deep in the Maritime woods. He loved his books, his log cabin and his garden, his peace and his quiet—and most of all his afternoons spent immersed in fixing, tinkering, and inventing to the delight of all. To the townsfolk who came to sit in the glow of his pot-bellied stove to drink sweet, hot tea and tell stories, he was known as Grampa Joe.

"Our Joe," they'd say, "you really are the most respectable, charming old fellow in all the county." And that would make him smile.

In fact, whenever anyone in the village did anything especially nice or polite or thoughtful, they'd get a friendly pat on the back and a *"You're a right Old Joe, you are!"* It was a compliment of the highest order.

"I'm an old man now, after all." He kneeled next to his bucket, wiping his brow. "Been a long while since I been tested, but I couldn't ask for better than this day, this sunshine, these weeds just as they are, right here among all that's mine and good."

With those words still loose in the air his heart lurched. *It's a mighty noble thing to be properly settled. I had my turn at adventure, and that's more than most can say.*

What he didn't know on that particular morning, as he bent again to yank the hawksbeard that dared invade his onion patch, was that a young boy stood just three fields over on the brink of something entirely unexpected. And that

EVERYTHING WAS ABOUT TO CHANGE.

Later that morning at the farmers' market, Mr. Stewart called out as Joe passed through the crowd with his bicycle.

"Hey there, Joe!" he said. "Can you come over later with your tools and your thinking cap?"

Joe cut through the crowd to the Stewarts' table. "What's up?"

"Well the peacocks, you know, they're mighty put out by the dugouts we gave the goats," explained Mr. Stewart, stacking tubs of yogurt. "I think we might please 'em with a new runaround, you know, something raised up along the roofline of the hut…"

Joe nodded, his curiosity peaked.

"Like a tunnel, you figure? I'd make it open-air, with ramp-ladders. They'll be able to tease those goats from up high…"

Mr. Stewart grinned. "I'll ask Anneke to bake a batch of those chocolate crackle cookies you like and I'll see you later, for supper?"

Joe waved over the heads of the townsfolk, his hands already tingling for his toolbox.

People end up with peacocks thinking they'll be this lovely adornment when in fact, they're quite particular indeed. So peacocks and peahens too big for britches landed one after another at Eric's family farm from all over the country and were given names like Paddington and Perry and Petunia and Paxton and Prescott, and they nipped and charged at anything or anyone who dared cross them.

What kept the Stewarts in the good graces of all, despite the squawking that carried for miles on still days, was the cheese and milk they brought to the market every Saturday courtesy of Gaetane and Germaine and Gaultier and Gabby, a crew of goats even crankier than the peacocks.

The only things the beasts of the Stewart homestead shared were beady eyes and a mutual dislike. And so the two camps tormented one another and thrived with constant bickering, the family so good-natured that they shrugged off the racket, insisting it was better than cable television.

On this market day the peacock shed was filled with the scents of fresh-cut wood, clean hay, and the steamy warmth of animal life. Insects buzzed, and a distant bleating punctuated the air over the meadow. Eric sat with his legs dangling over the edge of the hayloft watching Joe as he worked, a light breeze playing through the open window. The boy, lit up for several weeks with the revelations of his secret spyhood, fixated nervously on the lock of hair at the top of Joe's head as it undulated back and forth through the air like a snake to a charmer.

"So you're an expert in all things, ahh…pirate, then?" said Joe between throws of his hammer. Eric scanned the old man's face for mockery and saw none. He'd known Joe for as long as he could remember—for vocabulary homework one night his dad had used Joe as a point of illustration for the word *eccentric* and since then, Eric had felt in his bones that Joe was a grown-up to be trusted. And so, with the dried earth of his discovery still fresh in his nose, he had decided he'd held his secret long enough.

"You could say that," Eric said cautiously. "I haven't got much yet in the way of how they're organized, but I do know they're all over, and all sorts, and they're almost impossible to track even though they leave such a mess behind…"

Joe considered each word.

"And you've found things that you figure belong to these characters?"

"I have," replied Eric simply.

"But no sight or sound yet?" Joe rested the hammer on his knee as he looked up at the boy, fixing his face as earnestly as he could. Eric shook his head.

"I think they might be headed back this way. From what I can tell, they're going in circles. It's like they're looking for something. But we're off to visit my grandmother for the next few days, and who knows where they'll be when I get back…"

Joe rose to his feet, dusted off his hands and stood eye-to-eye with the boy.

"So, then. What will you do when you catch them?"

Eric startled. "When I…when I what?"

"When you catch them—you know, when you come across a clue one day and it's in the shadow of a…of a ship, as you say. What will you do?"

The suggestion of it emptied the boy's cheeks of all colour and Joe thought to himself *Good grief, he really does think he's on the trail of something. Pirates, in these woods? Impossible. There's nothing but an ocean o' farmland in this boy's line of sight…it's high time he gets out of his head and into the world.*

Joe looked downward, giving the boy a moment to compose himself.

"Well you know, pirate trackers tend to be…l-l-loose cannons, unpredictable." Eric gathered courage as he went. "We never know quite how we're going to get along until we're up to our necks in it, you know? I'm just going to follow my gut," he added, pleased with himself.

"Good man, good man." Joe reached up to give the boy's foot a friendly tussle before gathering up his tools. If not good sense, he saw industriousness in the boy—and misdirected industry was better than none at all. "Trust those instincts. That's the number one principle of spywork, did you know that?"

Thirsty for an icy mug of lemonade, Joe stood up, wiped his brow, and turned towards the cabin. It was the following Tuesday. Sunshine dappled through the raggedy jack pines, and swallow song and cricket buzz filled the air. He inhaled deeply and smiled to himself with great satisfaction, earth and sweat clinging to the creases of his hands. It was one of those All-Is-Right-With-The-World afternoons, his very favourite.

Knocking stakes along the edge of his tomato patch, a strange movement caught his eye. Without a breath of breeze, his tallest heirloom plant had begun to tremble uncontrollably.

"Well now, what's this?" he muttered, scratching his head and taking a step towards it. "How strange."

As he knelt to investigate, he felt it—a growing explosion that surged through the ground and up through the soles of his boots. The air stirred as the sound of crashing boulders and cracking trees and crunching wheels rumbled louder and louder still—imminent ruin on a collision course with his beloved retreat.

"What in the name of—" His chest leapt to pounding. Danger was thick in the air, too thick for time to think beyond *Whatever it is, it's not good...*

The forest began to shake from the direction of the north knoll, spitting crushed rock and splintered branches into the sky. He bolted out of the garden with his hands pressed over his ears and when he reared up on the small girl who stood in his driveway out of nowhere, he had to leap clear over her to avoid a head-on crash. Gravel spat out from underneath his feet as he skidded back round, his eyes wide with alarm, the forest crumpling around them as though it had been rigged for demolition. And yet there she stood, unmoving.

Before he could voice one of a dozen questions that clambered frantically at the bottleneck of his mouth, she spoke.

"Have you got anything to drink?" She spoke with a slight impediment, all the corners of her consonants rounded. Small, glinty eyes peered out from between sheets of pin-straight hair that hung on either side of her face like two halves of a door. She wore waffled long johns and someone else's steel-toed boots and a long tunic made of strips of salvaged canvas, and she'd be strawberry blonde after a few baths, all peaches and cream, the kind of girl you'd think came from a place that smells of lilacs and salty breeze. As it was she was the colour of nothing in particular, or the presence of dirt in the absence of all the rest—yet, he thought fleetingly, she didn't seem to care.

Sighing and holding his gaze, she spoke once again as if addressing a small child. "I've been walking a while. Have you got anything to drink?"

He sputtered a bit and she shrugged, turned, and walked up the steps of his cabin, humming to herself. Then her spell lifted and once again all he could register was imminent doom, and rather than following her as hospitality demanded he thought *Hide, man, anywhere!* He spotted an old soda-pop crate on his work shed porch, and he scrambled across the yard and up the step with seconds to spare. The rumble was upon him now, deafening. He dove into the crate with a clatter and yanked an old canvas overtop just in time.

Something told him, as he crouched, shaking, that the apparition who'd sauntered out from the guts of an explosion would find the lemonade on her own.

It was dark inside the crate. Joe held his breath and clutched his knocking knees, compressing himself into the tiniest possible old-man ball. Outside, the clearing exploded as the rumble arrived.

"AIAIAIAIAIAIAIEEEEEE!" screeched a chorus of voices above the cracks and pops of an engine that sounded like an army of unmuffled motorcycles. And then it all stopped. A great whoosh of steam was released and the yard erupted with heavy thunks and dragging shuffles and unloading heaves.

Joe couldn't help himself. He had to look. He lifted the canvas and leaned towards the edge, pressing one eye up to the sliver of light.

In the bright midday sun, an enormous hulk of a contraption as big as a barn (the thing that thundered, he supposed) had come to an abrupt halt in his front yard, sputtering and wheezing. The forest strip from where it came had been mowed flat, and a storm of stirred-up sawdust, pine needles, splinters, and smoke clouded the air. A rotten stench wafted into his nostrils through the cracks in the crate.

He saw figures through the stink and the dust, poking and rummaging and stomping about. Big, mean-looking folk, faces smeared with brown and swamp and soot. A pair of them bent hungrily over his freshly tilled garden, using shovels to dig up manurey, goopy mud and plop it into a vat on wheels.

"What do they want with all that slop?" he whispered to himself as he took in the scene. "That's about the muddiest-looking bunch I ever did..."

Then he saw it. A skull and crossbones on a torn black flag fluttered in the breeze above a greasy, sour-looking fellow who sat astride a battle cannon, kicking one foot casually against a trigger pedal.

It can't be…the boy was right? By god, the boy was right!

With shaking hands he fumbled in his back pocket to reach his *Indispensable Forest Almanac,* a regional compendium that commented on all manner of local phenomena. Contorting in the dusty gloom he thumbed through the battered paperback to the "Common Pests, Plagues, & Other Calamities" chapter, in which he strained to read an entry he'd never noticed before, sandwiched as it was between "Corn Worms: Insatiable Invaders" (he'd never grown corn) and "Pine Beetles: Ravenous Raiders" (his land was mostly firs and poplars)—

JUNK-HUNTING WOOD PIRATES: A CATASTROPHIC RARITY

Once thought to be legend, Junk-Hunting Wood Pirates go on rampage from first thaw to first snowfall. A menace to all gentle folk, Junk-Hunting Wood Pirates are notoriously cranky, mean, warty, rude, noisy, foul-smelling, and badly mannered. In constant search of junk, mud, and mischief, this loathsome bunch is said to ride recklessly through the forest in a giant mechanized wheelbarrow-ship, demolishing everything in its path.

Junk-Hunting Wood Pirates ransack the property of unsuspecting citizens in search of raw materials, scrap, mechanical odds, food, shiny trinkets, and other supplies, flattening anyone who crosses them with a blast from their Gooperator, a powerful mud-cannon. An encounter with Junk-Hunting Wood Pirates will surely ruin crops, squash pets and other loved ones, trash homes, and generally ruin your entire day. AVOID JUNK-HUNTING WOOD PIRATES AT ALL COSTS.

THE ALMANAC WOULD LIKE TO THANK THE REGIONAL UNSOLVED CRIMES DIVISION OF THE RCMP FOR THEIR LIMITED SHARING OF FINDINGS RESULTING FROM ONGOING INVESTIGATION.

"Eh! Vince! I betcha I gots us some ginger fizz, right up 'ere…"

Clutching the book in shock, Joe's stomach churned as he felt the shuffling of boots on the porch steps. The shadow of a giant hand passed overhead and Joe was near-blinded with light as the canvas was lifted. The last impression he remembered, before he passed out, was of sweaty socks and sewagey swamps and stinky cheese and week-old lobster shell compost. It was the most repulsive reek he'd ever smelled in all his whole, long life.

Chapter Three

IN THE COMPANY OF HOOLIGANS

"*Back* off, Phezzie," Joe heard a distant voice growl, feet shuffling around him as he came to. "Yer a bit riper today than usual, eh? We need this ol' coot to spill the goods, not lie there like a limp fish knocked flat from festeriness."

The smell cleared a little and Joe felt a pair of massive hands hoist him up to his feet.

"Old man!" hissed the voice. "You best come to if you know what's nasty!"

Slowly Joe opened his eyes and saw a mass of faces, twisted and strange. They peered and jeered at him, all crawly worms and rats' tails and bulbous warts and gummy grins.

"Who…who are you?" he stared, eyes wide.

"Who we is? WHO WE IS?" snarled the leader, a rhinoceros of a man with clever, fiery eyes and grooved skin and a beard like a tangle of burnt moss. *A towering tree himself,* Joe thought, *taken live with the crazies and come to crush me under its trunk.*

"Dis old feller says he ain't never heard of us, thugs!"

The madness circled more tightly around where Joe stood shaking. "We's the DREADS! We's a tempest o' trouble, a ravagin' rumble, a bomb-yeh-t'rubble, THA'S WHAT WE IS!"

(Following, dear readers, is a complete roster of the WOOD
PIRATE DREAD CREW as noted on the top-secret
WANTED bulletin board at the Lunenburg County RCMP
detachment. The existence of such a gang—confirmed through
years of near-encounters and undercover work—would incite
widespread panic, hence the restricted status of the investigation.)

Captains, Lieutenants, and Officers:
BEWARE the following RABBLE. Note the
DISTINCTIVE features of each VAGABOND.

Captain HECTOR GRISTLE has a beard and waist-
long dreadlocks the colour of dried moss, affecting the
illusion of snakes, as well as a complete disregard for the
values of noble, just, and fair citizenship.

First Mate Vincent the VILE keeps a colony of maggots
in his facial hair and is regarded as a formidable
strategist. Despite a lifetime of criminal behaviour, he
has never been apprehended.

Jury-Rigger WEDGIE Reggie suffers from chronic
eructation and dyspepsia, resulting in near-constant
flatus and epic belching. His primary role involves
rapid-fire repair work with found and stolen materials.
Secondary station: crew comedian.

Navigator SCREEMIN' Meena is completely bald, her skull covered in oozing warts of an unknown diagnosis. Not speculated to be a talent in the science of route-finding, she is said to rely on instinct, and dispatches coordinates when the (extremely loud) ship is in motion.

Machinist FUNKY Phezekiah is said to have not bathed in many years, and thus does not accompany the crew on ambush or downwind-facing missions. He is assumed to be in charge of engineworks and all metal moving parts.

Coxswain FETCHIN' Gretchen, hailed as the ugliest pirate of all, with chronic facial pustules and six toes on one foot, is in charge of the Brutes. She works with a bale of stinging devil's club lashed to her back, and is said to use it, and is also said to have very little patience.

Brute Ewsula THE BARBARIAN wears a necklace of rat tails and is the largest of all the crew, far beyond record books. Her origins are unknown. She is one of three brutes on crew for sheer muscle power.

Brute FAMOUS Amos cannot pass a mirror without stopping to admire himself—an exploitable weakness during pursuit.

Brute IRONBOUND Ike has no tongue. His wordless shouts are said to cause little or no communication barrier among the crew. We are informed he repeatedly charades the means of his accidental tongue amputation, but so far all attempts to recreate the incident have been reported as incomprehensible.

Of Knotjack CRANKY Frankie virtually nothing is known. A comparatively non-threatening companion has been sighted on-ship and is rumoured to be the crew's ropemaster, but upon undercover questioning, another crewmember insisted that legitimate pirates would never be heard to exclaim "Twist my knickers!" during raid or pursuit (investigative conclusion: pending).

Huckster ILL Willie Cusson is in charge of tricks, disguises, diversions and booby traps, although it is believed that successful stunts are more happenstance than skill. He appears to be the smallest of the crew, but makes up for his diminished stature by blowing things up.

Logdriver Johnnie GOLDEN is a wood engineer. During ship breakdown, his orders are said to be paramount and followed without question. He is also rumoured to be the crewmember with the most colourful language (no small feat).

Slopjack Zeke THE GREEK Popadopoulos is rumoured, by necessity, to be a master scavenger. He is afforded one gigantic pot, one gigantic knife, and one gigantic stirring spoon—a simple 2x4 with a scooped-out end—which is also said to be used upon the backsides of crew who hover as he cooks.

Gunner SLIMEBUCKET Sam, a toothless sack of skin and bones, is believed to hold one of the most esteemed positions onship—gunner in charge of the pirates' most feared and loathed weapon, the Gooperator. He is also rumoured to be its inventor, but this has not been verified.

Upon sighting:
1) Note any DEFINING CHARACTERISTICS that may aid in APPREHENSION
2) Calmly instruct all citizens in the vicinity to RUN
3) RUN*
4) Keep RUNNING
5) DON'T STOP
6) Report the incident IMMEDIATELY to superior officers including last known coordinates
*DO NOT ENGAGE without at least three complete regiments of mounted officers on standby (body armour and slime-repellent face shields mandatory)

"AIAIAIAIAIAEEEE!"

Joe's ears rang as the pirate mob screeched in approval.

"Y'can take yer pleases an' yer thank yous an' yer bran flakes an' yer daisy baskets an' go an' STUFF IT!" hollered a greasy, cannon-riding pirate. They shook their fists and cheered, pressing against one another, jostling and stinking, leering at him.

"We're beastly beasts, the dreadly DREADS!" shrieked another, a lady-rampager, her head picked bald and covered in warts. "Yeh knows us now, eh old feller? Look at 'im shakin'!" They roared with laughter.

"Get off, back to where you came from..." Joe shouted in vain through the melee. "Leave my home and my garden alone!"

"Getoff! Getoff!" they taunted.

"Scaredy geezer, poopin' skeezer!" screeched another lady-rampager, wiggling a handful of prickly spiders under Joe's nose and cackling as she popped one into her mouth and went CRUNCH.

"Break it up, crew, break it up," growled one of the largest, his hands in the air. "Hold him. Time to take stock."

As two of them moved forward to restrain Joe the rest scattered, put to task. They stampeded through his home, his barns, his garden hut, and his root cellar, upending everything within arms' reach and calling out yeas and nays. After some time a deep voice called out definitively and a pirate came around the corner of Joe's cabin, dragging his fingers lustily along its outer bark. He was the blackest, tallest man Joe had ever seen, with a sheen not of exertion but of a yellow dust, of the grinding of wood, and he advanced now with a confident swagger to where Joe stood frozen with his captors and their leader.

"Captain," the man growled, "this here cabin's the prize o' this place."

"Go on, Golden," the captain nodded.

"Logs of old-growth eastern white cedar. Uncut, unspoilt."

The pirate paused for effect, rapping his knuckles on the cabin wall.

"Captain, white cedar's been extinct in these parts for a hundred years. We'll salvage it, sell it. It's worth a thousand times more in pieces than as a hut for this ol' geezer."

The captain contemplated for a moment, then gestured approval.

"Done. Take it down," he declared, and the others gathered with sledgehammers and handsaws in a dismantling formation at each corner.

"STOP." The old man found his fortitude, improvising as was his gift. Several heads turned. "Salvage law says that prior to a salvage attempt, the salvor must receive permission from the owner unless the property has been abandoned..."

Upwards of a dozen twisted faces stared at the small old man in bewilderment, shocked at his presence of mind, which no ordinary person ever had, being too busy either cowering or running to speak. The captain's eyes narrowed into slits and he towered over the desperate figure of Joe, flanked hopelessly by brutes.

"There is no abandonment here, nor permission given." Joe's outrage picked up steam. "These logs were cleared for this cabin by my great-great-uncles Andreas and Philip, who came here all the way from Germany to walk to New Brunswick and back to rescue a herd of drifting Acadian cows. Those two were the first true salvagers of Sponagle Hollow. You are speaking to their direct descendant, and one who takes salvor's law for the rule it is."

"Any salvor removing goods has the passage of the Receiver of Wreck," the captain growled.

"Ah, but only before 1910," replied Joe, one finger in the air. "The 1910 Convention found the Receiver of Wreck to be corrupt and unethical, and it was disbanded..."

Several pirates snorted derisively.

"Lookit how much 'e knows," sniggered a pinched, sooty-looking one before a censorious glare from the captain.

"Never you mind the finer points of what law says we can and can't do." The captain pushed one finger into Joe's shirtfront and shoved with each word as the crew assembled at his back. "We are here. And we will take."

They pressed and they bullied until Joe tripped over the threshold of his work shed—the only outbuilding not yet explored during the pirates' sussing out of the property—and he fell on his rear end with a thunk. The doorway was filled with howls of laughter at the sight of a red-faced Joe sprawled on the floor, and all seemed lost. Then, hungry eyes adjusted to the void beyond—to bounty on a scale that made no sense given its modest shell, as anyone would be shocked to crawl through a mouse hole and find a palace that scraped the sky.

In future times, pirate folk would insist the Dreads wildly exaggerated the terrific sight that lay before them that day at Sponagle Hollow. But the tales were true: Old Joe was the keeper of the most staggering hoard they'd ever seen.

Chapter Four

ON THE FINE ART OF FLY-CATCHING

As the greasy, sour-faced one whistled appreciatively, the captain himself shouldered his way through the crowd to darken the doorway and even he, well versed as he was in the art of thuggery, went wide-eyed at the sight. There were stacks of metal sheeting, and rows upon rows of refurbished small appliances. There was a mountain of used tires and inner tubes, a pallet row of light fixtures to be rewired, and discarded furniture in need of new rungs and springs. An entire wall of reclaimed flooring and windows and construction material stretched into unlit darkness. *Shed* was a word wholly inadequate for what contained all this.

"Great—jumpin'—JUNK!" The captain lifted one boot and then the other over the threshold of the doorway.

"Not junk." Joe sprang to his feet and patted the dust from his apron. "It's found treasure, it is. Someone doesn't want it anymore, so I fix it up and pass it on. Simple as that."

Rolling ladders and swinging pulleys kept the bounty all in place, every last scrap stacked to the ceiling and pulled back with nets. Notes on masking tape read *needs stripping and sanding* or *replace motor* or *good for fort-building*.

"We live for junk," the captain murmured. The crew followed his lead, stepping inside and spreading out tentatively, pointing and gawking in wonderment. "We raid it, we claim it, we build up our Barrow, feed the bottomless gut of the union Reds. A pile this size would get us back in the black…"

Joe slunk back from the mob for some clear-headed figuring. *Me and these pirates are in the same business. They're recyclers, plain and simple. But they go about it in a way that makes them a menace.*

"How'd you score all this, old man?" The captain turned to grasp Joe by his scruff. "It takes my crew all season to rob a hoard half this big. We wants your secrets! Every roar and every grumble, every sneak and every rumble. You best show us what you do OR ELSE."

Joe was frantic as the snarling pack closed in tighter. *Let me get this straight…they like my junk…they want some of the same… they can't figure out why I've got more than they do…*

Then it hit him. Forgetting himself, Joe blurted, "For crying out loud, you're all thick as last year's potatoes. Everybody LIKES me."

They stared, struck dumb.

"I troll the yard sales, and the seconds bins, and best of all the annual spring cleaning garbage pickup, and I help all the contractors. But mostly, people come to me. They drop by whenever they've got something curious or tired or broken. They know I can make it into something, or pass it on to somebody else who could use it. That's it; that's all."

A stout pirate broke the bewildered silence with a long and juicy belch and Joe startled, almost laughing in shock, his fright falling away as the others traded confused faces and shrugs.

"I'm pleasant," he spoke softly, feeling a rootedness as he went. "I keep my woodstove stoked on a chilly day, and my neighbours come by with rhubarb muffins and whoopie pies. They like me because I share my tools, and my time, and my harmonica."

"Ahh, I do likes me the odd mouth organ…" The impulsive nod of a small, almost neat-looking pirate was reprimanded with glares from the others.

Joe pressed on. "My dear mother told me—and I've always found it to be the truest of all truths—*you catch more flies with honey than vinegar.*"

Hector "The Wrecker" Gristle, Captain of Calamity, leader of the dreaded Dreads, faced Joe with hands on his hips, the pirates at his back clustered like a hive of smoke-stunned bees. It was a revelation. The sheer magnitude of the bounty before them brought the prides and perils of nasty living—and the scope of its winnings—up for debate.

The captain was silent for a long time.

"Honey? That sweet stuff what prissy folk like…" he looked up to take in the bulging nets that hung from the rafters and the crew followed suit, pointing and gasping in continued awe.

"Can't be so…" he said, more to himself than to Joe. "All this and fer what? Cause yer…*nice?*"

"More or less," Joe nodded.

"But you're jus' one old coot," scoffed an enormous, barbaric-looking lady. "You've not got a crew, no one for to rough it out?"

"Just me," he said. "They call me Grampa Joe."

"D'yeh jus' ask folk for stuff, and they…'aaaaand it over?" belched the stout one, a dribble gleaming on his chin.

"So long as they don't need it anymore." Joe raised his voice to be heard at the back of the crowd. "And so long as I smile, and say *please*, and *thank you*, and *good day*."

"Out, all o' you." The captain waved a dismissive hand over his shoulder and the crew shuffled wordlessly though the door and into the yard.

They were alone in the shed—the most pleasant, upstanding man in Barss County and the most ruthless hooligan in all the province. The captain dragged two stools into the centre of the dirt floor, kicking up a cloud of dust, and motioned for Joe to sit. The concentrated scowl on the pirate's face pressed Joe to accommodate.

"Tell me everything," he demanded. "Start from th' beginning."

Pinned to his seat by the force of pure charisma, the next hour was the longest of Old Joe's life so far. He told the pirate captain of how he'd started out as a tinker, a travelling handyman of sorts, whose ticket to adventure came by way of earning the favour of good people. There were the Inuit who taught him how to make his own kayak and follow the whales;

the forest keepers in Bella Coola who brought him to their
old-growth treehouses to count the grizzly bears far below; the
tuna fishermen of Saint Margaret's Bay who shared their skill
until Joe could row their dories through the roughest swell. All
in exchange for his usefulness, his good nature, and his handy
ideas.

Gristle listened intently, his brow furrowed, chin to fist.

Joe told the captain the secret of his life, the thing that
every single one of his adventures had taught him: that *being
nice is always more profitable than being nasty.* That helping
other people, and working hard, and having clever ideas and a
cheerful disposition make people like having you around. So
they make you chicken fricot and blackberry buckle, or show
you something new, or help you find your way to the next place
where you meet more friendly people, and help them too, and so
on and so on. And before you know it, you're everyone's beloved
and you've seen every corner of the country.

When Joe was done, his throat was dry and he felt quite
parched, although his nerves were strangely still. He couldn't
help himself. After a pause, he spoke once more.

"What about you? How'd you end up here, Captain, sitting
in my shed?"

The next hour was the shortest of Old Joe's life so far. A
reluctant storyteller at first, the captain revealed how he went
from poor boy to pirate. Joe sat rapt, forgetting his predicament.
Despite horrible manners and a thunderous temper, Gristle had

lived a life much like Joe's—one full of breathtaking excitement. But it came about in a sad sort of way. All his life, no one had ever been nice to Hector Gristle. Not once. Not ever. So he grew up big, and strong, and cranky, the only way he saw to make his place in the world.

After he gathered his crew, they became sanctioned by the international union (Joe didn't dare interject for details, as much as he wanted to) and the newly christened Dread Crew lashed out farther and farther afield. They built the Barrow and the Gooperator and took whatever they wanted from whomever they crossed. While Joe collected new friends everywhere he'd been, the captain and his thugs collected new enemies. It was a prickly, unwelcome life.

"Don' know what I'd do if it weren't for my mates." Gristle tugged at a knot in the tangle under his chin. "They all been lost or left like me. Now we roll together, us an' our Barrow. We got each other but it takes a toll, it does. Takes a toll. An' if we keep not makin' quota, we'll all be—" the captain stopped abruptly as if remembering his station as well as Joe's lack of it, and he shook his head.

A strange peace settled over the work shed. Then from outside there was a sniffle, a whispered curse, and a chorus of shushes, and it occurred to Joe that the entire crew was perched on the step, straining to hear through the door.

How bizarre... Joe contemplated the captain, who suddenly seemed a little more ordinary. *I'm being attacked by thieving pirates, yet my gut tells me it's about time to break for a jug of malt cider. Something tells me this Hector fellow'd like the kick of it.*

"Tell you what." Joe had made up his mind. "I've got an idea."

The captain, lost in his memories, looked curiously at Joe.

"How about I teach you, and you teach me?"

Hector Gristle blinked, stupefied for the second time in his life.

"I could help you and your crew learn how to...not make so much of a ruckus. How to get people to like you, maybe, or at least not mind you. Then you'd find it easier work to get what you want, to get the places you need to go."

"Hmph," grunted the captain, not altogether in dismissal. "Honey lessons. And in return?"

"You let me tag along," Joe blurted, too fast to think.

The old man took a split second to consider his own recklessness. This gang was a rowdy terror, that much was plain. But Joe, not being inclined to heroics, wasn't intervening for the sake of good folk everywhere. He simply couldn't abide inefficiency—it grated on his nerves to see fuss where there need be no fuss. *There's no shred of cleverness in a blind rampage,* he thought to himself. *Things ought to be sensible. I am a fixer, I am, a fixer of broken things, and that's all.*

He took a deep breath.

"I love my homestead, every inch of it, right down to that old soda pop crate. But I could use a bit more adventure now and then, you know, like the old days. To keep me young."

Joe felt oddly shrewd and purposeful. The captain studied him carefully, noting the change in the air but unable to put a finger on what it all meant. He stared deadpan at Joe, then stood up and cupped his hands around his beard-buried mouth.

"AAAIEIEIEIEIEIEIEIEEEE!" he shrieked. Joe near jumped out of his skin and the door burst off its hinges as the rabble took its cue.

"SIR YES SIR!" they bellowed in unison.

"Lads and gals," he said commandingly, not taking his eyes off Joe. "We have ourselves a NEW RECRUIT!"

The most ear-splitting roar of the whole day erupted then inside the shed. The crew swarmed around him, scrambling to introduce themselves properly and slap him on the back. Then he was lifted off his feet onto broad shoulders and a throng of whipping, grubby louts, out the door and into the next chapter of his life.

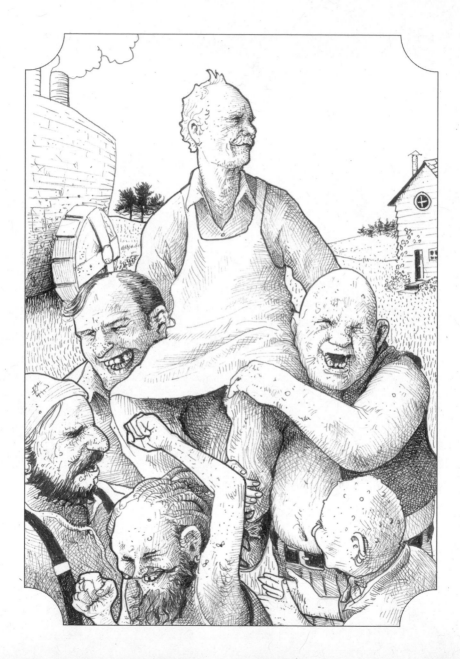

Chapter Five

THE NEW RECRUIT

Grampa Joe was not frightening in name or persona. He grew fiddleheads. He washed between his toes. He slept with a crunchy buckwheat pillow. He liked order, and sensibility, and his eggs sunny side up. Not piratey at all. Not in the least.

He stood there before a jury of beasts and bullies feeling very sheepish indeed. Gristle scratched his beard, contemplating the recruit. It was a glorious moment, for a pirate. It was name-time. Propriety-shedding time.

"Speak up, crew," muttered the captain. "Think quick, and think nasty."

They circled closer, whispering and murmuring, their eyes dragging up and down the decidedly unassuming character put before them.

"Errr...how 'bout *Jalopy*? *Jalopy Joe*?" gobbled Gretchen, her chins wobbling. "Worn out, rough 'round the edges, like?"

"Nahh. Not threat'nin' enough. Anyone else?"

"*Jackboot*!" burst a voice from the back. "Like a puffed-up, pantsin' bully, right?"

"Like me ma used to call me," the captain nodded. "Gettin' there..."

From the heart of the huddle, Joe's eyes fell on the barbarian-lady who stood fingering her rat tail necklace, her face screwed up with intense thinking. *You've got to hand it to them,* he thought, overcome with irrational fondness. *They certainly take this business to heart.*

"I'VE GOT IT!" roared the captain with a start. "You are: *THE JACKAL!*"

The crowd hummed with approval.

"I, uhhh…the what, sir?" Joe halted. "Like a…like a dog, you mean? I had me a Duck Toller when I was a boy. Had the fleas something awful, not bad at catching a frisbee. Used to eat spoonfuls of peanut butter. I don't quite see the… uhh…"

Gristle lowered himself until he was eye-to-eye.

"You don't see?" he sneered. "You delinquent, dawdling drifter! You no-good, loafing stumblebum! You ragabond of vagabonds! You should be PROUD of such a glorious name! To take the name of the Jackal is to be the ultimate LACKEY OF DISREPUTE!"

The captain grinned wide like a sliver of moon in a coal-black sky.

Joe the Jackal…how depraved. Not the sort of person you'd invite for Sunday supper. Despite himself, Joe smiled back.

"Yes, sir!" he cried. "Thank you, Captain, sir!"

He yelped as the brutes Amos and Ike lifted him onto their shoulders once more to jostle and bounce with a view of the whole scene—his tiny cabin, his trampled garden, a giant, wheezing woodship, and a crowd of cheering pirates.

What a morning, thought the old man to himself, feeling all at once brand new.

A cheer is more punctuation than sustenance. Before long the pirates were once again occupied at their stations, either accustomed or indifferent to Joe's presence. Beyond the marvels in his shed, the Jackal did not yet belong.

Joe spent the afternoon wandering aimlessly from giant to giant, peering around shoulders and asking questions that were met with grunts and noncommittal shrugs. Finally he stood lost at the middle of it all, unsure of what to do with himself. He took account of these adoptive comrades, his mind a jumble of names and impressions. The barbarian-lady— Ewsula, she was—grumbled rebelliously with the speechless Ike while Johnnie, the tallest, blackest man, barked at them about a log pile he needed stacked. There was Screemin' Meena bent over a map, muttering to herself before flipping it the other way round and scratching her head. Cranky Frankie was easy to remember, being so at odds with all the roughness that surrounded him. He floundered atop a mountain of tangled rope ("Carry on, Jackal...fit as a fiddle here, toodledeedoo!") while the small Acadian they called Ill Willie scampered out the galley porthole after a series of minor explosions from within. *Something tells me those blasts will be all daisies and sunbeams compared to the wrath of the cook finding out Willie was muckin' around in his kitchen*, thought Joe, rightly.

"Like crackin' into a social club for porcupines, eh?" a small voice spoke from just behind him. It was the curious girl who had a knack for popping up—the young greyhound lithe and spare in a company of weathered, ragged oxen. Joe turned, took in her slight figure, and sighed.

"Fair enough," he agreed. "A porcupine motorcycle gang. One of those real nasty ones that eats its own every second Tuesday."

She smiled and said nothing and just then, Joe decided he liked her very much.

"Who are you?" he asked plainly. Now was no time for the usual manners.

"I'm Missy," she replied. "Missy Bullseye. That's the name they gave me, and I like the last part best."

"Indeed." Joe sensed the girl's name was well earned, although he wasn't yet sure why. He smiled and just then, Missy decided she liked him very much. And so they sat on the ground with legs crossed, and there she told him her story.

As the Barrow thundered past one stormy afternoon, she had leapt from the branches of an apple tree, grasping through the slick downpour to a frayed bit of rope that trailed behind the ship.

"I've got no family, none that I can remember. I worked for food at the cannery, then the dory shed, then the sail loft, but whatever my blood, the sea's not in it." She gestured to her ears. "I don't hear too good, you mighta guessed. Don't matter. One day I felt a rumble in my feet like I never felt before, and ten minutes of running later, I seen 'em, and they was headin' inland like bats up a chimney, and somethin' told me to just grab on, and hold fast."

At the next stop she was discovered, an unbidden stowaway. The captain growled *This ain't no place for breakables, MISSY,* but she stood her ground with her hands on her hips, windblown and caked with mud. *I'm here, like it or not,* she had replied defiantly. *Nothin's broken me yet.*

Then Vince, the first mate, appeared soundlessly at Hector's side. *Girl's got spunk, give her that. She may well be useful. A decoy of sorts, a go-between. She can be the sheep's clothing for our pack of wolves, so to say, yeh?*

And so young Mairi was granted shipboard, addressed as Missy with a hint of scorn to remind her of the propriety she'd been born to, that which branded her an outcast until proven otherwise. She persisted, skulking in shadows, and in one sticky situation after another she would emerge and neatly turn around a near-disaster.

You just passed the turn, she'd call, her voice ringing like a bell above the cursing, the growling, and the yells. *Keep going this way and you'll end up at the old quarry, and I don' care how monster these wheels are, you'll get socked in at those gravel piles sure as quicksand.*

And so Mairi became Missy, and Missy became the indispensable Missy Bullseye for how she always quietly succeeded no matter what.

"Can you hear at all?" asked Joe.

"Not much," she said frankly, as she said everything. "It's always been muffled but I pay attention better than anyone else, and payin' attention turns lip-readin' and good sense into more than enough."

No doubt, thought Joe. She dug her fingers into a pocket, retrieved a hardened hunk of something that looked entirely inedible, and chewed the end of it contemplatively.

"If anythin' I should thank these plugged-up ears, and the Dreads should, too," she continued. "From where I stand that Barrow purrs like a kitten and the ogres drivin' it, too. Nothin' bothers me. They were pretty peeved when they picked me off the end o' that rope, but then they seen I'd be useful, and that was that."

"Useful? But you're so small," said Joe before he startled, not having meant to speak his thoughts aloud.

"That's right," she said, as though there was nothing more appropriate than for a young girl to be small, and to gnaw contentedly on bark jerky in the aftermath of a pirate raid.

The weeks passed and Joe was threaded into pirate life more with every day. It was an intermission of sorts, a pause in the rampage that allowed the Dread Crew to tend to long-delayed projects and ship maintenance as they studied Joe's ways, the Barrow tucked neatly next to a remote barn and looking more like its unremarkable twin than anything else. One by one the

crew came to trust him, and consult with him, and include him
in pranks—the pranks in particular marking the end of his
probation and the beginning of his belonging.

"Going off on an adventure again, I am…won't be back for
quite a while," he'd casually mention to whomever stopped
by the meadow gate—the mail lady, the seed delivery boy,
the bewildered pizza man who staggered up the path one day
under the weight of five dozen specially ordered onion-jalapeno
calzones. With every deceit he winced, especially to think of
the boy three fields over who watched the woods with such
justified fascination. But at the bottom of his spine he felt that
something bigger was to come of it all. Something worth the
necessary scheme.

Before long, the whole village put off tea and whoopie pies
in his absence, thinking the place deserted. Joe—Jackal Joe, that
is—was simply so sweet, so loved by all, that even a takeout
order big enough to feed an army passed without suspicion.

"It's that Stewart zoo at the farm next to his," they said. "He's
always bringing the goats treats, giving them improper cravings."

While his every morning was spent giving Honey Lessons
to the crew in the secluded back field—"The Silver Lining
of Asking Nicely," "Sharing Can Be Profitable," and "The
Undiscovered World of Occasional Bathing"—his every
afternoon was spent learning the ins and outs of crewing.
Scrubbing the scuppers, high-speed disembarking, twisting
the last tuft of hair on his head into a knotted lock. Despite

never bringing himself to stir his soup with Ewsula's rat tails, or crunch black widow spider legs, or pick his nose at breakfast, Joe had begun to blend with previously unimaginable rabble.

Occasionally someone would take him aside, show him a trick or two. Vince would holler for "some git" to bring him a refill of pond slime and Joe would scramble round the corner, bucket in hand, to assist in the greasing of the wheels. Opportunity was simply a matter of keeping ears peeled and being ready for work, for Joe a truth as elemental as clouds that make rain.

Joe was shaken from a deep sleep with rough hands. It was Sam.

"Up! Up!" Sam exclaimed as he whipped Joe's blanket onto the floor. "No time to waste, no time. Weather's come up and you got the Barrow this night, you did! The Barrow!"

Within seconds of opening his eyes Joe was thrust into a midnight downpour for every recruit's most telling initiation— his shipman's trial. He'd hovered in the shadows of the Barrow's undercarriage, peering into its mechanical guts whenever he got the chance. Every night he went to sleep with it crunching through his head, its tarry, smoky whiff in his nostrils. The pulling of this duty was a milestone, a mark of trust.

What a bundle of nerves and shakes he was, bursting out of the cabin on Sam's heels, instantly drenched. All self-respecting pirates bristled at being branded "pork-on-the-planks"—un-useful, dead weight, slowing the rampage. *Please, oh please,* whispered Joe to himself as he stumbled down the path, willing himself to snap to it, *please don't let me be pork.*

The woodship was smartly concealed next to the barn and behind a wall of flowering vine where the pirates were encamped. Each morning they'd wheel it down to the clearing behind Joe's cabin, dousing it with leech oil to keep it slick despite the growing summer heat.

The crew was up tightening ropes and double-checking knots, unfazed at the relentless darkness and wet, and the ship was coughing green-black smoke as the engine loosened and stretched. Phezzie looked up as he crouched at the cogs and announced with a wide grin, "Look here, lads and gals! The pilot of honour shows his dirty mug!"

As he entered the fray they almost knocked him off his feet with a chorus of advice and encouragement.

"Easy on the skipper-clutch my boy, easy on the skipper-clutch," rasped Vince, his arm draped over Joe's shoulder. "You can let her loose if you've got some speed, but in close circles you'll want to go it easy…that is, unless it's a hot day and the jigger's backed up…"

Vince retreated and Ewsula, the barbarian, took his place. Her encrusted braids knocked against Joe's shoulders. "Go long and hard on that clutch, Joe!" she insisted, rapping his chin affectionately with grubby knuckles. "Hard as you can—get her goin'!"

Joe gulped. Sam's voice rang out above the storm and the mob scattered, resetting under the shelter of the cabin deck.

"Skipper up!" he hollered.

In his life Joe had scrambled up the halyard lines of tall ships; spelunked through tunnels and caves; and flown, forged, and rowed his way from one end of the country to the other. Nothing compared to this. Hand over hand he climbed up the mounting ladder, the crew rapidly dwarfed far below. Having scrambled over the edge of the pilot's perch, he stood at the wheel, the view at his back like being suspended over the edge of the earth, the stern of the ship sweeping down abruptly. Laid out in front of him, the deck was littered with a tangle of rope and forest flotsam. He saw the junkhole—the chasm that led to the hold—and the engine seat, and the companionway leading to hammock upon hammock in the sleeping quarters.

This is their home, it suddenly occurred to him, as his eyes travelled over the splintery, worn-through hardness, the rampant brown. *It's all they've got.*

"Eh!" yelled Gretch over the chug of the engine, and Joe peeked over the edge to look down on them once more. "You waitin' on a permission slip?"

They all chuckled, resting companionably far below and chewing sticks of bark jerky. They thought him too soft for such a beast; he knew it.

"'Member what I told yeh," cried Sam, a little too shrilly. "Don't go too easy on 'er, she stalls if yeh don't get her revvin' good. Two strokes, three maybe, then just let them chompin' wheels bust their own path, mate! We got thunder cover, so no ears fer a hundred miles would raise alert. Don't stop fer nothin'…"

The spectators shook the planks of the cabin steps, stamping and pumping fists into the air and gesturing frantically, but Joe could hear nothing over the ship's growl.

It was time.

Chapter Six

A TINKERING OF THUNDER

Three fields over, Eric stared at the ceiling. His eyes traced the ribs of the old house, counting square-pegged nails in an effort to sleep as a restless wind lashed branches against his window. He sighed, dejected. *These old beams feel like the inside of a ship…*

For a long while there had been clues everywhere. On nearly every expedition he'd either stumble onto a flattened track of forest that stretched as far as he could see, or he'd find a piece of litter that made no sense in his world, or he'd see a headline that broadcasted PIRATES! to anyone clever enough to see. He tracked evidence on the county chart, noted as thumbtacks formed patterns and predictability, felt a growing confidence in the craft of his spywork. Then, famine: all clues vanished.

The forest restored itself, broken swaths sprouting green with fern and moss. And as calm spread throughout the woods, Eric's frustration grew—for a spy without a target was nobody at all.

What would I do if I caught them, anyway? Turn them over to the police?

C-C-CRASH.

A pitter-patter on the roof, and the skies opened.

Should I have some kind of weapon? Nah. Maybe a badge...

C-C-C-C-C-CRASH.

Again, thunder shook the sky, and Eric flinched.

Yikes. That one was close.

C-C-C-C-C-C-C-CRASH.

The thunder escalated to an unbroken rumble. Eric rose from bed and reached in the basket for woolly socks made by his Great Auntie Jean, who had never been one for humility when it came to knitwear, deeming hers the "best socks east of Ontario for when the weather's owly and the stove's gone to embers." And they were.

No one'll sleep through this racket. I'll put a log on in the kitchen, boil some water for mom's maple tea, sweeten her up...

With Eric's spyhood stalled, he'd decided to ask his mother for a chore-free morning to pay a visit to Joe, to seek advice from the only other soul in on his secret. On his way downstairs he stopped at the landing window to catch a glimpse of what sounded like a chorus of explosions. There was another crash, yet through the glass he saw nothing but blackness.

Thunder without lightning? That's weird.

He shrugged, rubbed his eyes, and padded towards the glowing crackle of the wood stove where his mother already sat in her robe, smiling, with her hands wrapped around a steaming mug of maple tea.

C-C-CRRAASSSH.

With a throw of the crankbrake the Barrow lurched forward into the downpour and the exhaust backfired with a bang. Joe wound the clutch in a desperate bid to keep it from stalling, pumping the accelerator as hard as he could.

Then the ship woke up. Every plank and rope tensed with obedience like a pack of sled dogs poised for a good, long run. Joe yanked on the landline and it came loose, dropping in a tumble at his feet. Then he was moving and could scarcely believe it, giddy as rain pelted his cheeks. One previously ordinary man, he was, perched atop what felt like a horse barn, an ironworks shed, several junkyards, and a few compost heaps all thrown together in a monster mash of epic proportions. He felt more unproper than he'd ever been in his life, and better for it.

All this and he hadn't even broken through second gear. He flattened the same strip of meadow grass round and round, the honour of being at the helm lending the illusion of thrilling speed.

"Whooop!" he yelped, triumphant, unable to contain it. "AAIEIEIEIEEEE!"

Over the edge of the pilot's perch he saw them long before he heard them. They stood in the light of the cabin deck, the whole crew on their feet, pointing and…wait…*laughing?*

The tailpipe sputtering, he coaxed the hulk back towards the spectators, who were now in hysterics. With a great, final shudder, the woodship fell silent as Joe threw landlines to the upturned arms of Sam, who grinned broadly far below.

"WHAT'S-SO-FUNNY?" he yelled through cupped hands.

"You!" cried Sam. "My granny could spin circles around you! No, my granny's dog! My granny's dog's granny! Yer slower than all of 'em put together!"

Shimmying down the chain net, Joe landed in the saturated muck of the meadow with a squelch.

"This is all my land, round here," he protested, making his way through the steam and the storm to where the crew snickered and shook their heads, arms crossed. "If I get this ship up to speed, it's going to demolish everything in its path!"

Willie rolled his eyes. "*C'est le* 'ole point, *ami, non?*"

Panting with exertion, Joe took a moment to scan the group. Gristle fingered his beard while Reggie muttered in his ear. Vince, maggots twitching, snorted at a snide comment from Gretchen. Johnnie and Sam argued the finer points of Joe's cornering while Amos, Phezzie, and Zeke sat together in a puddle with a tin of crackled curry-twigs, faces heavy with unspoken opinion.

"Consequences," said Joe firmly. A few faces turned to him inquisitively.

"CONSEQUENCES." All eyes were on him now. "Being all honey means being tuned in to what sort of footprint you leave on the world." He gestured to the ship at his back. "This footprint—it costs you."

It was Gristle who spoke first.

"We's old dogs," he replied as the others nodded solemnly.

"Noise and ruckus, that's what we know. We're a ravagin' rumble, after all. Not a whimperin' whisper."

Joe was stern. "You want more stuff, more junk, right?"

At this, the grumbling quieted.

"It's *stealthy* I'm after, and *stealthy* doesn't have to mean un-piratey." The idea formed in his head as he spoke. "Figure out how to make this Barrow purr instead of chew up the woods, and she'll be the toast of the town wherever you go. Why, they'll be swarmin' around you like scamps to an ice cream truck!"

Joe had stretched beyond himself to earn his new name—he was skilled at slime harvesting, a quick study at knots. He'd even come to appreciate the sting of cracked nettle root, grinding enough on each meal to make every pair of eyes in the near vicinity water profusely. In a matter of weeks Jackal had propelled himself from inconvenient to tolerable to street-credible to genuinely useful. And in this company, usefulness excused all manner of petty grievances and missteps—for usefulness was the currency of respect.

But this? A tiptoeing woodship? The idea wasn't merely odd. It was outlandish.

Joe's moment was dashed by a call for late-night slop and the crew retreated to the dry warmth of the galley, shaking heads and mumbling amongst themselves, leaving the old man deflated in the tail end of a storm.

Sam, the Barrow's chief mechanic and gunner, was so devoted

to the ship that he'd stay up all night long trimming stray splinters. But Sam wasn't on watch for the rest of this night. Reggie was—and Reggie was notorious for sleeping on the job, especially in the relative safety within Joe's gates.

When Joe crept around the corner and past the wall of vines, he found the ship deserted aside from Reggie's peacefully slumped figure at its base. Eyes brightened with the prospect of tinkering, Joe rolled up his wet sleeves and picked his way through the grass to the great wooden hulk, whispering to it like a skittish horse.

Let's see, you and me, he cooed through the pre-dawn gloom. *Let's make you so slick, you'll slip through the woods like whipped cream off a slice of warm pumpkin pie.*

The ship exhaled at that, weary of crashing and bashing. He crept past the starboard bow wheel, the tip of his monkey's fist dread knot barely reaching the height of the hubcap. Crossing the loading ramp, he shivered at the damp gust that yawned out of the cavernous hold. Finally he climbed a spare rope ladder and made his way up to the engineer's platform on deck—Vince's post, as first mate—and unscrewed the steel plate to reveal the ship's whirring guts, its clicking insides, the very brain of this woody mammoth.

Tracing the lines of an imaginary grid to keep track in his head, he noted each knob and tube and slider and bolt, all the domains of propulsion, navigation, and anchoring. Finally, he saw it—the smashplug—the automatic route-finder that steered the way as the forest exploded all around, the crew hanging on by the skin of their teeth. Through the gloom he peered through the indicator window—thick with rust and gunk it was, never having been adjusted—and saw it was corroded, frozen to STRAIGHTLINE BASHING.

Hmph, thought Joe. *That sure doesn't bode well for whatever gets in the way. It can't be this simple…but why not give it a try?*

After chipping at the rust with the edge of his pocket knife, he tugged briskly and the whole smashplug popped out of the joint with a faint *schwuck!* and came loose to rest in the palm of his hand. He stared at it feeling he was on the brink of a moment he'd always remember, like the changing of a season lit by the first sparks of brazen red.

Slowly, thoughtfully, he turned the plug head to end and inserted it into the joint backwards. It clicked into place and a soft *whirrr* emitted from the engine—a change of heart in a living, breathing beast. With his chest pounding, his eyes found the indicator again as its arrow now swung smoothly to rest on EASY DOES IT.

Chapter Seven

THE UNOBSTRUCTED ROCKET

"You want to go and see Joe? But he's not around much these days, they say." Eric's mother padded across the kitchen floor in her slippers to collect the mugs from the table. It was almost dawn, and the storm had moved off. "Anyway, we're headed to Shediac to see the cousins. It's the lobster festival; did you forget?"

He had forgotten. It was one of the best days of the summer—fresh corn and buttery claws and strawberry shortcake, and then the lights of the midway, the Scrambler and the Zipper on the edge of an endless beach—but right this moment, all Eric wanted was to sit on Joe's stoop and talk spywork.

"Right. When we get back, then. Maybe Joe'll be around when we get back."

Eric shuffled upstairs to bed for whatever remnants of sleep could be had and his mother stared after him, perplexed.

Joe had raced back to his cot three feet above the earth, or so it felt. As dawn broke he lay fully dressed, waiting for a second

chance at the helm—a chance he'd have to orchestrate on his own.
I'm about to hijack a pirate ship. He waited for the sun, giggling
under his quilt in a manner not remotely befitting a pirate.

A soon as the birds chirruped the new day, he flung the
quilt off and sprang lightly to his feet. The creak of the screen
door was amplified in the misty closeness of dawn, and he drew
his breath in through his teeth before closing it inch by inch,
fearful of a slam. Down the steps he picked his way through the
front yard, a respite for the crew, all of whom took advantage
of the peace of Joe's land to sleep in open air rather than in
the cramped barracks on ship. Stepping over barrel chests and
minding his feet as he went, he balanced like a tightrope walker
through the tangle of limbs and snorts and grunts and slack
jaws. As he crept away from the circle he muttered an apology
under his breath at the sight of the captain—the only one to
sleep upright, Hector sat against a tree, his closed eyes the only
sign of rest for a body alert in all other appearances. Free of
the circle Joe broke into a sprint, his feet padding the ground
silently, through the lupins and across the courtyard to the barns
where the Barrow awaited him. He was clear.

CLINK.

CLINK.

CLINK.

The chain net jingled and rattled with every step as he
climbed—an alarm-raising, he realized, too late—and Sam was on
his feet before his eyes were open, stumbling towards the ship and

rousing the others to do the same. Joe increased his pace as curious figures approached and his window of opportunity shrank.

"Jackal—izzat you? Not duty call yet, why the aboardin'?" Sam's face was confused as the others collected at his back, rubbing eyes and stretching. Now safely over the edge of the deck, Joe strode towards the perch and took the helm, one hand on the wheel and one hand on the crank.

"I've got something to show you," he called, and before any of them had a chance to blink twice he hit the ignition and knew—his modifications had worked. *WhhhhhhiiiiiRRRR!* the ship purred and the whole crew startled, deeply suspicious.

Sam turned to Hector in protest and was met with a silent, breath-holding wordlessness. Phezzie, his coveralls tied down around his waist from sleeping, stepped forward looking almost frantic.

"Somethin's up with the unmuffler, she's on the fritz...and look, the muck belt's on the wrong way..."

"Blast it all, that boltplug's too tight, and that one too..." Johnnie arrived at Phezzie's side, wood's counterpoint to his metalworks. "A few good crashes an' they'll both crack, and that'll strip the bark off the popper..."

Before any of them could reach the ladder, Joe eased the ship away from the crowd. Through the rising smoke he could make out some figures gesticulating wildly, others frozen in shock.

Then BAM! Joe and the Barrow left the pirates in a cloud of gravel spray, shot like a rocket down the old logging road at the west edge of the potato field. Beyond the rolling of wheels on soft earth there was no grinding, no cracking of boulders, no mulching of trees.

"Nothin' but leaves in the breeze." Sam was all disbelief as pirate after pirate rose to scour the trees. "Like there's no ship at all, when no one for miles should be able to hear themselves think…"

Shoulder-to-shoulder the crew stood stunned, Phezzie and Johnnie bickering anxiously. They'd never heard so much of… *nothing* from the Barrow. Not ten miles out, let alone on the very same stretch of land.

"It's not fittin'," grumbled Vince sideways, leaning confidentially towards the captain. "He's gone and done somethin' to the rumble, and we're in trouble enough as it is without the union gettin' wind o' this…last thing we need is for 'em to see we gone soft…"

"THERE! Over there!" screeched Meena. They all swung to see…the *putt-putt* of the garbage truck making its way down the old highway beyond the gates.

"Here he comes!" Zeke dropped a load of freshly squashed leeches he'd been carrying in his shirtfront. "The rustling way by the pond!" And at that a mischievous flock of crows burst from the willows, cawing and cackling.

"Shush, the lot o' yeh…" hissed Gretch. "Maybe Jackal's learned a thing or three from us, yeh? Maybe he's GONE, taken our ride, off to steal our stealin'…"

The pirates were chest-to-chest now, bickering in distress at the disappearance of their most curiously misbehaving ship.

Then a *WSSSSSSHHHHHHHHH* of steam at their backs whipped dreadlocks into the air and the pirates spun round to face a panting ship and a beaming Joe, who stood at the bottom of the zip-pole (stretching from the pilot's perch to just above the ground, the zip-pole was for high-speed disembarking during ambushes or in moments of great excitement, of which this was the latter).

It was Hector who spoke first, pressing his way through the crew to reach Joe.

"You've got explainin' to do, Jackal, and don't you try me or it's hold-scrubbin' duty for a month," he snapped.

"North Mountain and back." Joe was smug. "Clear as a bell."

"Impossible!" sputtered Sam.

"Malin comme un cric!" In his shock, Willie's tongue lost its English.

"Just now?" the captain shushed the others. "You weren't even wearin' yer rockplate, I seen that much. But…mother o' badness, that was fast…"

"That wasn't just fast, Captain, sir. That was unobstructed. Nothin' in the way." Joe scanned each pirate in turn. "Two things: first, she needed a tweak here, a fiddle there. Now she's…gentler. Second, there's hundreds of abandoned railways, logskids, and forest access roads that'll get you everywhere from Bedford to Bella Bella. Let 'er use 'em! Enough of all the crashing. Get around faster, less mess, less upset..."

The crew exploded in outrage.

"No mess? No upset?" shouted Sam. "I built this ship, or the guts of it anyway, *for* mess and *for* upset! We bump up against the world an' we like it that way. What d'yeh think we are?"

The mob roared.

"...Lambs at a pettin' zoo?!"

The mob roared again.

"...Doorbell-ringin' milkmen?!"

Reggie screeched "KNOCK! KNOCK!" in a mocking falsetto and the crew erupted into howls of derision. Joe said nothing but kept his eyes fixed on the captain, who stood scowling and fingering the unruly scruff on his chin.

"They're right," Hector muttered as Joe strained to hear him. "Union won't have it. Rulebook says we're to be feared. That's how you rustle up more for the drops. Where did that rulebook get to, anyway? VILE!"

"Union? What union? What rulebook? What drops?" Joe tried in vain to keep up with Hector, who'd turned from him and pushed his way through the crew in search of his first mate. He left Joe to deal with a noisy airing of grievances, every brute and engineer from Amos to Zeke clamouring to demand that Joe put the Barrow back to rights.

As late as midnight his ears rang with their distress. *What makes sense to me makes none to them, that much is clear enough*, he thrashed in his cot. *Where that leaves me, I've got no clue.*

Eric opened his eyes. *I think maybe of anybody, he's the one who might believe me.*

Five minutes later he was dressed and standing in front of the toaster, waiting for his bagel. *BING*. He buttered. *He's been here ever since the loggers left. He'd know what doesn't belong. He'd know where to look.*

Fifteen minutes later he lifted the latch to the goat shed and stepped inside to bleats and stamps. He set out fresh hay as he always did, oblivious this time to Gaetane's methodical chewing of his pant leg. *I told him about the Baby Slug Snax wrapper and I swear, I saw him smirk. Why would he do that? You don't smirk at proof.*

Two minutes after that he poured fresh water for the peacocks as they strode circles of impatience. He looked at his watch. *He might not believe me but he hasn't seen the attic. It's too early yet and who knows—Mom might be right. He might not even be there. But I've got to try.*

And so he waited, his eyes scanning the ridgeline for both a suspect and an ally.

Joe gave up on sleep. A faint glow from the porthole hinted at a hot cup with the early-rising Zeke and so he stepped into the galley, and sure enough, the stout, powerful man turned to him and nodded, glad for the rare company before breakfast.

As Joe rubbed his eyes and settled himself on a stool, the slopjack handed him a jug of junebug pepper tea, a delicacy Joe had come to think of as his morning kick-in-the-pants. As he cupped his hands around the clay and blew gently across the top, the pirate spoke.

"I been thinkin', y'know," said Zeke, kneading the day's soda bread, a secret recipe baked on the steaming surface of the engine block (*Grit's good for the gizzard*, he insisted). "I'm with you. What'd you call it? Un'berstructed? Seems sensible."

Joe smiled gratefully. "That's good of you, Zeke, but the others don't agree."

"Of course they don't." The cook slapped a hunk of dough onto a flat of plywood bound for the engine room.

Joe bent to sip his tea, watching Zeke's muscled arms knead and roll as he shook off his grogginess. A master scavenger, Zeke skipped the rampage for the sake of gathering, trolling the woods at every stop for ingredients. From floor to ceiling, the galley was stocked with his bounty—flats filled with pinned slugs for sun-drying, cheesecloth bags plump with junebugs, the black oil of mashed leeches in shatterproof mason jars, and netting that overflowed with leaves and fungi for steeping.

"Now there's a treat I know. Garlic scapes…" Joe pointed at a barrelful of shoots with curls of crisp white.

"Phezzie's favourite." The pirate slapped another lump of dough onto the plywood. "There's no peace from him durin' scape season. They give him a lift, but he shoots flames out o' both ends for days…"

In a cupboard behind a wire mesh door were heaps of raw caperberries tied with twine, bundled devil's club, stinging nettle, bitter dandelion, and crusted seaweed. Together they added a zest to the ship's staple: wormy tubers, a hardy, yam-like root vegetable that grew in raised mud beds on the foredeck of the ship. More bitter than sweet, with a rust-coloured flesh and gnarly skin, this everyday belly filler was as pockmarked as the pirates themselves.

"Some say it's Sam holds the reins o' this gig, him on the trigger, you know," Zeke said with a sudden edge to his voice that roused Joe from his observations. "Or Phezzie, keepin' all the metal in order, the engine parts. Then others say if it weren't for Johnnie, we'd be a pile o' splinters ten times a day. Then of course there's the captain, and no one dares pull a finger without his say-so."

Zeke looked over his shoulder conspiratorially.

"It's me." He was defiant. "I'm the one what keeps this racket goin'. I grow them tuber bricks what keep those bellies from whinin' all day long. Without me, this'd be a shipful o' lost lambs."

Another hunk of dough hit the plywood flat.

"Cap'n and Vince, they're the brains, and all the rest, the brawn. But you're the heart and the blood and the guts," agreed Joe, reaching for the tea jug. "That's how it is on every ship, you know, even in Her Majesty's Navy. The cook rules the ship."

Zeke considered this solemnly and then cracked his knuckles, satisfied.

"So tell me, Zeke," said Joe, leaning forward. "Seems you think I went about it wrong, eh?"

Zeke humphed. "First, yeh pulled that stunt with the Barrow right before sup. Those beasts were starvin' before you'd even set foot in the perch, and when they're starvin', all they're good for is raidin'."

"What else?" urged Joe, the gravity of his missteps sinking in.

"Wrong words," continued Zeke, after a pause. "Yeh said stuff that made it sound all…nice-like, what you was tryin' to do. Y'shoulda said *wily* and *sneaky*, yeh?"

Zeke's fists pounded the last hunk of dough and with a poof of flour it joined the rest. The cook turned to Joe then, studying him for a moment before nodding briskly as though he'd made a decision.

"On with it, then," he said gruffly, cinching his apron and slapping his palms together. "Let's stuff these thugs so thoroughly they'll tap dance for yeh, if y'ask."

"What?" Joe slid off the stool onto his feet.

"Tuber brekkie pie." He moved through the kitchen with surprising grace given his size, reaching into one cupboard after another until a pile of ingredients lay on the table. "Brekkie pie with raw garlic, aged blue cheese, egg milkshakes…near a month past due. Nice an' skunky. Look here, I've even got eight pounds left o' roach bacon—should be almost enough. Make that meself, I do, an old recipe that one is, yeh mash 'em into a loaf first then slice an' fry…"

Joe was emboldened as the first light of dawn seeped through the greasy portholes. *I've just earned my first ally. One down. Thirteen to go.*

Two hours later the pirates lay heaped in a state of comic indulgence, belts loosened and sighing contentedly. Joe sensed his moment and willed his pounding heart to subdue itself.

"Beggin' your pardon, Captain," he said evenly, picking his way through the bodies to the stern of the deck, where Hector reclined with his boots up. "We need to talk."

"That we do," the giant replied, and an alert sort of listening rippled across the deck from one crewmember to the next.

Joe took a deep breath.

"It's only me who knows how to undo what's been done."

Zeke nodded in discreet encouragement from the back of the crowd and Joe felt his feet root to the deck. The curious silence deepened.

"You've got no choice but to give it a try. If your take doesn't suffer, no harm done. If it makes things worse, I'll undo it all, put her back to rumblin'."

The whole of the crew tensed in unison, recognizing the rock and the hard place between which they were stuck. Fuming, Vince rose to stand in front of Joe.

"You mean to do as you please, presumin' to take tools to our ship, then hold us to it?" the first mate growled. "This is against code. This is against the chain of command. You, recruit, are so far over the line you're nothin' but a speck on the horizon."

A rustle broke the silence and then Missy was on her feet, her face steely.

"He presumes 'cause he's makin' it up as he goes, just like a pirate." She spat her words, hot with frustration. "You get so braggy, the lot o' yeh, sayin' 'The mother of invention is insubordination!' and then along comes Joe to push out all your edges, just as well he should, an' yer whinin' about rules. I say if you're not ballsy enough to give his way a go, your world's only gonna stay the same or shrink."

My word, her moxy, thought Joe.

The bickering escalated, as did the friction in the air. Pirates took sides and dug in, barking all manner of barbed foulness at one another.

"DREADS!" Hector roared, and it all stopped.

"SIT," he ordered icily. They obeyed.

"Vince and Bullseye are both right. What's done is done. We work with what we've got. Union won't like it, but we've outrun them before."

Again with union talk. Joe had a hundred questions, none of them to be satisfied.

"Everyone, back to work. Engineers, I wants all you at th' panel—you too, Jackal. Take us through what yeh've done and we'll make do, and who knows. Your tweakin' might need a tweakin'…"

"CODE RED!"

Missy's frantic shriek rang out from the bow pulpit and heads turned to look at the source of her pointing—a lone boy who strolled confidently along the deer path and down the slope towards the cabin. Joe grimaced.

Blast, it's Eric Stewart. He's coming the back way so he's not seeing the closed gate and the mail I've let pile up…

"I'll handle this—just a neighbour—right then, let's hoist that shield…"

Already tucked behind the horse barn, the Barrow needed concealment only on the side that faced Joe's yard. The brutes pounded across the deck, shimmied down the chain net, and ran to the pulley to hoist the curtain of greenery into place. High above, the rest of the crew went still, frozen on the planks of the deck.

"Joe? You here?" the boy's voice called out and Gretch, Amos, Ike, and Ewsula gaped in dismay, exposed in the open with no time to make ship.

"The root cellar!" Joe hissed. The four giants dove headfirst through the hole in the grassy mound and Joe slammed the wooden door shut behind them with a clatter.

"There you are." Eric rounded the corner, hands in his jean pockets, and hopped up on the front step of the cabin. "What's up? Got any lemonade? I'm thirsty."

Joe, panicking inwardly at the disarray of the yard, was dumbstruck.

"I'll go have a look." The boy let himself in, calling from the pantry as he opened cupboards in search of mugs. "Been so quiet I was startin' to wonder if you'd gone off again…"

"Nope, just…well, I mean, yes. Yes, that's right." Joe hurled a canvas over the pile of Frankie's ropes, shoved Meena's charts under the picnic table, and kicked Phezzie's reeking boots over the threshold of his tool shed. "Had to go away, and then errands, and then away again…nothing exciting, nothing at all…"

The boy appeared on the porch with a glass of lemonade in each hand. He paused to cast a quizzical glance at the old man, who stood wide-eyed in a cloud of stirred-up dust. Eric inhaled and grimaced.

"Pheeeewph, Joe! What stinks?"

"Ah! Yes indeed." Joe scratched his forehead. "My…ahh, my boots…thrown in the compost by accident. Didn't know till I went to turn the bin. They've been stewing in there half the summer. Got 'em up on the roof for a good sun-bleach."

Eric blinked. "Must be some boots."

"Took me to the Yukon and back, you know." Joe reached for an offered mug and nodded in thanks. "Not much honour in letting 'em be done in by lobster shells and slimy lettuce, right?"

He took a long gulp as the boy studied him thoughtfully.

He seems jumpy. Eric turned from Joe to gaze around the yard, lifting the mug to his lips.

BRRRAAAAAAP.

A juicy, luscious belch erupted into the air above the barn and Eric whirled back to Joe in shock.

"That was SICK!" He howled with laughter, almost dropping his drink.

"'Scuse me. Falafels for breakfast." Joe sunk his head in mock embarrassment.

"This kid in my geography class can make it to the letter P," Eric chattered. "He tried it in the spring talent show and got sent home, it was great…"

I've got to get him out of here. Now.

"So Eric, I'm curious." Joe set down his mug. "You'd said you've been tracking these…what did you call them? Pirates?"

Eric snapped to attention. "Yeah right, Joe, but lately…"

"Show me, won't you?" Joe interrupted him. "I've done some spywork myself, you know. Maybe I could help."

"Really?" the boy was saucer-eyed.

"Sure. It's been too much back-and-forth lately, and I could stand for a puzzle right here at home. What d'you say we have a look at what you've got so far, and while I'm at your place I can finish that peacock run for your mom and dad. Two birds with one stone, Eric. Always a good thing…"

As the two walked through the yard and towards the field, Vince, crouched on deck to peer through a crack in the hull, narrowed his eyes. *That boy's going to find himself up to his nose in it,* he muttered, and he was right, as usual.

Chapter Eight

SHE WHO TRACKED THE TRACKER

"*People* are going to be here soon," Eric's father called through the attic hatch. "Let's hang the sheet on the barn before it's dark, and we need extra butter before the store closes, and come and help me get the projectors lined up straight…"

It was a few days after Joe's visit to the attic, the eve of the family's annual Midsummer Movie Marathon. By the glow of a bonfire the whole village would turn up with woolly blankets and lawn chairs to take in the classics in smoky open air: epics, mysteries, slapstick, and science fiction salvaged before Liverpool's old Centennial Theatre met the wrecking ball. Each year there were great debates as to which films would be wound onto vintage projectors, and invitations were sent out announcing the all-night lineup. Eric's job was to mind the unruly creature that his dad had brought home on the back of his flatbed truck—an antique popcorn maker with brass piping, circus lettering, and a mind of its own.

Later that night Eric scooped in a cloud of fragrant steam, handing out bulging paper bags with one eye on the flickering screen. If he left the popcorn maker untended it would spill kernels like lava, and so when he noticed a flicker of light in the attic window he kept stirring despite the panicked lurch in his gut. Nobody ever went up there. Nobody but him, that is. And Joe, the other day, who had listened intently to his theories but said very little in response other than "Keep your eyes peeled" and "Oh, I forgot to mention, I'm hitting the road again tomorrow, won't be back for a few weeks."

He scanned the crowd. All his family and the usual troublemakers were present and accounted for—some engrossed in the movie and others tussling in the hay piles, jacked up on the novelty of staying out late. A few more clustered round the bonfire with marshmallows and mugs of hot chocolate. He glanced furtively at the attic again—a shadow, movement. Someone was up there. Someone who did not belong. His hideout was breached.

"Simon!" he whispered. His partner in Ms. Durling's social studies class turned to him and Eric gestured at the popcorn crank. "Take over here for a second, will ya?"

Simon shrugged and rose to his feet, his eyes still on the screen, and took Eric's place. Eric pounded up the first flight of stairs, then the second, then the third. As he reached for the rope to pull down the hatch steps he hesitated, regretting the tumbling ruckus he'd made on his way up, and watched wide-eyed as nimble footfalls above sent tufts of dust through the cracks.

Now or never. He unfolded the steps and popped his head

up to see a well-travelled pair of steel-toed boots in front of his face. He looked up.

It was a girl—a girl in a grimy tunic and long johns who stood poised as though she'd been expecting him. He tore his eyes from her long enough to note the open sailmaker's chest, its false bottom slid open and its contents rifled, and the light upon the county charts. He climbed up through the hatch to stand in front of her and they appraised one another wordlessly before she spoke.

"You're a tracker," she said, a glint in her eye, and Eric was struck with the oddest sensation of being in the gaze of an X-ray, all his secrets laid bare. He lowered his face.

"You could say that…" he mumbled, staring at his feet. "What are you doing up here?"

She said nothing in reply. He looked up at her to find her staring intently at his face at his mouth—with exasperation.

"Look up and say that again," she said sternly. He blinked and met her gaze.

"I just…I guess I am a tracker. And I want to know why you're up here."

"No matter to you," she said, speaking with a slight impediment.

She's deaf. Eric almost gasped. In front of him stood perhaps the most perplexing girl he'd ever met, her keenness not remotely dampened by whatever hand she'd been dealt. She was that much sharper for it, he guessed.

"Funny you're a tracker," she said again with a smirk. "I'm a scout." And he felt then like a peacock to her goat. *She was one of them.* How? Why? All he knew was that this small girl, his own age or younger even, had eyes as seasoned as old Joe's.

"Eric!" his father's voice rang out from downstairs. Eric startled and turned to listen. "The popcorn's overflowed and Simon and Poppy upturned the butter bowl…better get down here…"

Her eyes alight and fixed on him, the girl backed to the open window and sprang through it to the top of the roof ladder.

"You're close, you know." She gestured through the night air at the open chest and the bulletin board. "Closer than you think."

She grinned as Eric moved towards the window, but by the time he leaned out there was the rustle of branches and the soft thump of her feet on the grass below and she was gone. He saw the rope then, a crude thing with loopholes for feet, stretching from halfway up the apple tree to the roofline. And for reasons he would only understand after everything had come to light, he left it there in case the girl of the woods might someday return.

Chapter Nine

OIL TO WATER

Sam buffed the trigger—the only part of the ship that glistened—with a pristine piece of flannel. With Joe's words his movements slowed with distress and disagreement.

"Nothin' in need of fixin' when it comes to my Gooperator," the gunner grumbled after a silence. "Them prissy folk don' like bein' mussed up. They go half out o' their wits, runnin' and slippin' about, drippin' in my goop. Good sport, good sport. Anythin' else just wouldn't be fittin'."

Joe sighed. The ship's newfound stealth was one triumph, but its muck-slinging cannon made bullies of beasts—beasts who were more misunderstood than all bad, despite the stink.

The monstrous thing was ingenious, Joe knew that much. A barrel cannon with high-propulsion pistons, its vat swung like an udder under the belly of the ship, funnelling the juice of the sloppiest ditches, swamps, and noxious ponds into the bilge—and to that the pirates added the by-product guts of sun-dried slugs, maggot-infested tuber roots, Limburger cheese rinds, extracted squirt of skunk, lobster dung, and the odd pair of discarded long underwear that even Phezzie had given up wearing for the unbearable stink. The bilge fed the vat and the constant motion of the ship was a cement mixer, tending and tossing—the resulting goop emitting such a stench that a rubber gasket was installed to shield the living quarters and deck of the ship from the fumes of what lay stewing below. The vat then fed the cannon, which expelled its contents at a pressure high enough to pin any unfortunate soul under an avalanche of spew.

All of it lay in trust with Sam. Sprung by a feathertouch trigger that shone like the sun, the slimebucket was the Slimebucket's own to command as he pleased. And so Joe began his campaign of persuasion with him—only to be shaken off with a disbelieving snort. To suggest altering the Dreads' hallmark was unthinkable. Especially for its keeper.

Joe turned on his heel and went to summon the only one who might consider it—someone with a vested interest in collecting more junk more easily, to heck with the usual ways.

He knows they've got to change if they want a haul like mine.

The bow pulpit was the highest lookoff on deck, what seemed to Joe a quiet spot. The captain stood with his arms folded across his chest, having granted Joe licence to speak. From the trigger post Sam strained to eavesdrop, gripping his rag with white knuckles.

"It just can't keep on, you see," Joe pleaded. "That thing—it's built to upset people. You may not hurt their bodies, but you hurt their trust."

The captain studied Joe as he might study a bug, curiously, a fluttering diversion either easily squashed or easily spared for its pattern and promise.

"Make it some kind of...spectacle." Joe's voice grew steady. "Make it into something that makes people run to you instead of away, you see? Like fireworks or a piper in the open air. Make it so they line up to give you all the junk you'll ever need and thank you for the privilege."

Hector stepped down to pace across the upper deck, deep in thought.

"Been this way for decades," Hector mumbled to himself, his eyes on the planks as he circled. "Second overall, we were, three years running, no complaints. We was a mayhem and now what? Quiet *and* nice? We'll spend more time runnin' from those blasted bureaucrats than we'll spend junkin'. Union's not going to stand for this, and we're in the red as it is..."

At this, Hector seemed to shrink a little. He paled and cracked his knuckles, bristling with nervous energy. Could there be more at stake than the well-being of citizens? Was that fear on the face of a giant—fear of *bureaucrats*, of all things?

Despite a racing mind Joe said nothing, for it is the nature of a leashed pack of dogs to pull against restraint. Sure enough, the giant's natural disdain for authority won out with no more urging from Joe.

"This here gun brings in the goods," he declared, raising an open hand towards the cannon. "An' our bosses want goods. An' goods aren't known to be gotten wif' pleases an' thanks. But our bosses ain't seen the inside o' yer shed, Jackal. I have and so I'll heed yeh—but only to a point. There'll be no dismantlin' here. Take its teeth, but not its bark. Got it?"

Joe blinked as the challenge sunk in.

"Aye, aye, Captain." He masked his satisfaction behind a face of solemn respect and hopped down from the pulpit to walk the length of the deck past Sam, who gaped in shock. It was done.

Two days and three nights passed with the entirety of the gun, its barrel, its scoop shaft, and the underbelly vat all draped in canvassed scaffolding, the pirates circling like territorial crows. On the morning Joe finished he whipped off the canvas with a flourish like *ta-da!* and the crew clustered round in assessment.

"Doesn't look much different. But—look," pointed Johnnie. "He's put some kind o' strainer 'cross the sucker. That's gonna get clogged up with slugs in 'bout two seconds flat..."

Joe stood with one foot up on the trigger, grinning proudly and taking in the speculation with amusement. It was the refurbishment job of a lifetime.

"No, no!" wailed Sam. "He's taken out the solar foil, and now there'll be no way to melt the big bits so they don't plug the barrel...how's he gonna fit a good-sized dung pattie through that hole?"

Willie ran his hand along the network of chilled piping that now encircled the vat.

"Acid?" he said, hopefully. Joe shook his head.

"Nettle juice?" Joe shook his head again and reached down to crank the churner. Instead of unleashing a cloud of skunk, it misted an unusual, icy-cool violet vapour into the air and the crew gasped in unison.

"Is it POISONOUS?"

"Does it STING?"

"Can it BLISTER?"

"Nope, nope, and nope," Joe replied. "You'll just have to wait. Valuable stuff, it is, have to choose our moment carefully…"

The crew's protests were shushed by the captain, for Joe had won the right to patience, a thing even more rare than manners in company such as this.

"That's it," Hector snarled. "That's all you get today, like Jackal said. Back to your stations."

The pirates skulked away, casting scowls over their shoulders, and Joe let out a breath he hadn't been aware of holding.

The next day Joe pulled sandblasting duty with Ewsula and they sat together on three-legged stools, buckets of razor clams at their feet.

"How's a bunch like you kept in line?" asked Joe, reaching into his bucket. "No one's said. D'you get points? Penalties? Reports?"

"Bah," humphed Ewsula. "Me, I'm three-quarters genuine barbarian. There's no puttin' corners 'round that, now, is there?"

She chuckled, pleased with herself. "Captain strings us up a day or two when we get soft, throws us extra rations when we get good an' nasty."

"Rations?" replied Joe. "Besides wormy tubers?"

"Yeah, you know, treats," she licked her lips. "Beetle 'n' batwing pizza, worm whiz on swamp sticks. But the big one? That's the holiday, mid-summer hot dog day. We work all year long for that one day. We rest, we eat hot dogs. Hundreds of 'em. Thousands of 'em. Extra ration tickets on hot dog day…good as gold."

"Never heard of such a thing." Joe reached into his bucket for a fresh handful of shells. "I wouldn't have pegged you—I mean, us—as a party sort."

"Yeah," she shrugged. "We do mud-skidding on puddle boards. We play moss-chuck. We bob for apples."

"Oh!" said Joe, grasping at the familiar. "Always loved apple-bobbing."

She smirked. "We do it in a barrel full of wriggly worms. With cider apples left to rot. They get squishier that way, what with all the bugs."

"Or crunchy, if yer lucky enough to get a millipede or two," added a rough voice from behind them.

"Heya, Golden," Ewsula said. "Did yeh get that beam under the pulpit jammed back in?"

"Stinkin' thing's stuck." Johnnie pulled another stool over and heaved himself upon it with a groan, thick with dust and sweat.

"I'm gonna have to chop it all out and start new, but you know me. I always likes a good chop."

As Johnnie wiped his brow, Ewsula handed Joe a wadded-up piece of paper from the cuff of her sock. Joe unfolded it, resisting the urge to wipe his hands.

DREAD CREW 46th ANNUAL SUMMER HOT DOG SHINDIG

It's a hot dog party, there's no doubt—and if you ain't DREAD we'll scream GET OUT! We'll hang you from the scuppers! We'll drag you through the crud! We'll strap you to the mainstay and whistle while we tug! So you'll steer clear, if you got any smarts. You'll get out of our way, 'less your head's full of farts!

"Right," Johnnie snorted, leaning to look over Joe's shoulder. "There's some three or four hundred days in a year and all we get to kick it up is one stinkin' afternoon. It's that blasted union, 's what it is. They got us by the…"

Ewsula cleared her throat loudly and spat a chunk on the toe of Johnnie's boot. He shook it off, habitually unbothered.

"Tell me more," urged Joe.

"You thinks we're vinegary? Hmph. That lot's downright surly," he grumbled, unbothered by the barbarian's censorious glare. "Least we gets some laughs along the way and you know, we stick together, but them? Grim as the day is long, they

are, like gettin' an earful o' rusty tacks. That's always when the
Barrow gets it worst, when we're runnin' from 'em…"

Ewsula sat with her chin to her fist, the pile of razor clams
forgotten at her feet. Johnnie continued.

"They don' like us 'cause we do what we like. We almost got
caught that day Phezzie talked us into raidin' that cheese factory
instead of the sheet metalworks, 'member that, Ewsie? We
almost got caught three times from the nose-pluggin' stench."

"Who's in charge?" Joe leaned closer.

Ewsula sighed. "Chief B. Boss of the bosses, the bureaucracy,
we call 'em. The Reds. They call us scrappers and they don't care
how we do it, but we gotta keep movin', never stop. We rustle
up the junk and they break it down and sell it raw. Wood gets
chewed up and spat out for sheets o' beaver puke, what they call
plywood an' byproduct. Glass and metal and wire all gets melted.
We get the pick o' the rest."

"And if they catch yeh under quota it's housetoil—they
take yer ship and it's forced labour at headquarters," Johnnie
interrupted.

Ewsula shuddered and cursed under her breath.

"My cousin Lothar's with the submariners, they're under
the water up top of Europe, and they got tangled up in a
scallop dragger's net two seasons ago," he continued. "They
missed a bunch of drops, and they was already on probation
for not claimin' a bunch of prime junk—that's stealin' by union
reckoning. They's on housetoil. Right shaken up, 'e is. Ear-

bleedin' instrumental music all day long, and they make yeh wear suits and ties, can y' imagine? Pushin' paper, not a whiff o' outside. Lothar's almost done his term so I heard they posted him to the receivin' dock, which at least gets yer blood goin', but housetoil is…"

He drew air in through his teeth with a hiss.

"…*unnatural* for us folk."

"Why don't you just go off on your own, free agents?" asked Joe. "What do you need a bunch like that after you for? You're pirates, right? You're not supposed to answer to anyone."

"We're not about to set off adrift from all our other folk," Ewsula explained. "The union—they got spin doctors that plant stories and throw police off, smudge over any trace of us. They look after our fogies an' our sicks. They send news of all the others. We's scattered so much, the jungles an' the cities an' the water an' the mountains an' we can't know who's where without 'em. They're a pain, no doubt, and *yurgh!*"—she shuddered—"the last thing any of us want is to get stuck in a corner by 'em. But there's no union anywhere that'd take care of us the way they do."

Johnnie huffed and rose, knocking his fist against Ewsie's and then Joe's.

"I'm getting' th' willies with all this union talk. Catch you two later."

Ewsula and Joe paused, watching Johnnie disappear down the stairs to the hold. Then the piratess sighed, tossing her string of rat tails over one shoulder and revving up her blaster once more.

"Without the union, ordinary folk would close the gap, y'see," she spoke over the whirr of the blaster. "And we don't mix with ordinary folk."

We don't mix with ordinary folk.

Joe watched as the barbarian resumed her work, his part in the task at hand forgotten. *What a shame*, he thought as he watched her. *They're misshapen and gigantic and they smell terrible but they've got uncommon instincts when it comes to cleverness. What a shame everyone can't see what I've seen...*

He burst to his feet, sending a pile of unfinished shells to the ground with a clatter. "Pardon me..."

Ewsula scowled, jolted more by the nicety than the commotion.

"I'm off to find the captain, just remembered something I need to..."

"Suit yerself." She bent over her stool and Joe was gone.

Chapter Ten

BIRTH OF A SPECTACLE

Joe found Hector on the ground at the stern of the ship, engrossed in a pile of charts.

"Gristle!" he panted, skidding around the corner. "I mean, Captain…have you got a second?"

The giant grunted but didn't look up. Joe dove in, chattering at double speed.

"I have an idea. Just the thing to have us all swimming in junk for always. Ewsie and Johnnie just told me about the pirate holiday, the festive day, and I may as well tell you I know about the union troubles too…"

At that, Hector stopped what he was doing and shot a warning look at Joe.

"Here's the light bulb, Captain. Open it up. Get the townspeople to join in. I don't know what they'll think but they'll come, curious as they are. They'll come by the busload, I promise you."

The pirate searched the new recruit's face. Joe was genuine, his eyes bright with anticipation.

"It's for the JUNK, see." He paced, hands dancing. "A festival where everyone from all over can come to share ideas, and bring tired things, and tools, and paint, and find out who needs what and work together and invent new stuff...and eat hot dogs. And play games, too, wild, piratey frolic. Quite the novelty! Can't you see, Captain?"

"You try my patience, Jackal," growled Hector. "More than usual. I don't buy it. Even if I did, the Reds'd be all over us like stink on Phezzie."

"But..." Joe protested. The scowl on the captain's face stopped him cold.

"All our lives, people've called us a pox," he spat. "You think a bunch of hot dogs will cure all?"

"Anyone who didn't run from you would be completely mad!" Joe burst. "It's just...if you want to live a little easier, get more junk, well, that's why I'm here, right? Cause you're in some kind of trouble with this union..."

After a pause Hector nodded.

"Here's what I think," Joe continued, his hands waving through the air as he spoke. "Put the word out that the festival is pirate themed. Tell everyone to come dressed up, so you'll all blend in, and they'll let their guards down enough to see that you're all...well, rather genius, I'd say."

The captain raised one eyebrow.

"We tell everyone to bring as much junk as they can—to rejig, to trade, to invent and recycle and dispose of properly. That ought to drum up enough to get that union off your backs at least for a while, right?"

Joe watched as his words sank in.

"All that plus you'll get known as the most respected inventors and recyclers anywhere," Joe cried passionately. "Imagine if Brock, the mechanic down Rigaud way, saw the Barrow. He'd knock Sam off his feet with questions for a solid afternoon. And think of all that pesky scrap he's got to find a place for—worn-out snow tires, busted filters, mufflers, cracked transmissions…"

With that, a delighted peep escaped from nearby, followed by a chorus of unruly shushes. The captain turned and saw the toe of a boot hiding behind the vine curtain, and the shadows of many more.

"Come out, all of you," he sighed, and then leaned in to Joe. "I know they're not easy to crack into but ever since they seen your loot, they won't miss a word."

The pirates appeared one by one from the other side of the arbor, filling the space by way of all five senses. Sam wore a wide grin, obviously thrilled that Joe—and possibly others—would take the same joy in his charge as he did.

"We're sorry for sneakin', sir," said Sam. "This idea of Jackal's…it's strange, to be sure, but what have we got to lose? Other than a few extra dogs, that is?"

"We are some sore with all the pressure," added Phezzie, a cloud of raw onion sandwich wafting from between his teeth. "Nobody wantin' us to come 'round, always hidin' and sneakin' and runnin' from the Reds, it grates after a while."

"Soooore, some soooore," belched Reggie in agreement.

"Can y'magine?" said Meena, twiddling a tuft of frogs' legs between her fingers. "Pullin' up to some town and having them all there to meet us, wantin' to trade and give us stuff and take what we fix? Then maybe bring us somethin' hot and spicy, some Tabasco tea and dusty crunchits all ready for us, like…like we're not minded?"

The circle of pirates stood in silence as the imaginary scene washed over them. Crickets clicked in the grass under their boots, and the breeze rustled the leaves of the poplars above. Not a single one of them felt like stamping on flower beds or snarling at baby-tots and a confusing sort of sensibility rippled from one to the next, an unspoken tiredness and sudden longing for the welcome of others.

Seems to me the Dreads are worn out from being dreadful, thought Joe to himself. *Seems to me they're ripe for somethin' new.*

And so they were. After more discussing and compromising and debating and relenting, Captain Hector Gristle gave his fist-up to the First Annual Junk 'n' Joy Festival. The vote on the staging ground, the first task at hand, was unanimous. Joe's back field featured a gentle slope with soft grass, ideal for rolling. A glade full of tire swings at the north end. The duck pond on the west side, with its sandy beach and walkabout path.

"And a skunky little swampland on the east edge. I've got somethin' just right in mind…" chirped Sam excitedly.

It was a blank slate on which several hundred revellers could wander and frolic as they pleased. It was perfect.

The wooden screen door clattered shut and from his room at the top of the back stairway, Eric heard the squish of boots against the dirt floor of the breezeway that connected the old sheep stalls to the main house—stalls now scrubbed to shining and stacked with rows of spices and dairy strainers.

"Anneke—" his father's voice called out. "I've got something to show you...outlandish, you'll never believe it..."

Outlandish? Eric's hand propped up his chin as he sat upstairs at his desk, staring listlessly at a crude map of the old Christmas tree farm up the road. Planter roads, deer paths, logskids...he had to have missed something. They can't have just vanished. *I'll eat my own shorts if there's anything outlandish a hundred miles from here.*

"Sounds promising," his mother said, a smile in her voice. Eric eavesdropped despite himself.

"Found this under the windshield wiper of the truck just now," his father said as he crossed the room. "Can't for the life of me figure it's for real..."

From the kitchen there was a rustle of paper and then murmuring silence, and Eric instinctively slid off his stool and crossed soundlessly to the top of the stairs.

"Not another flyer," murmured his mother as she examined the mysterious find. "What on earth...Dreads? Says here it's a... what? A pirate fair?"

Eric tumbled to the bottom of the stairs like an upturned

sack of bowling balls and stared slack-jawed and breathless at the backs of his parents, who stood with heads together over a small piece of paper.

"It's to do with junk, or a jig, and hot dogs of all things." His father scanned the invitation. "And something called rockbeer, and a snack made of slugs, if you can imagine that—it doesn't make much sense, but apparently everyone from ten counties and more is invited. Says here it's happening at Joe's, can you believe it? Although he does have the most land of any of us... but he's been away, hasn't he? Seems it's being put on by some gang what calls themselves pirates, but then why would Joe have anything to do with it? I'm sure it must be some kind of prank..."

Eric's knees buckled and he reached out for the nearest steady thing , bringing an entire shelf of mason jars down with a shattering crash. He'd been right all along. He was a tracker, and his target had just invited the whole population of the county and the province and beyond for a picnic—*next door*. The concerned faces of his parents and the ceiling beams all swirled and blurred together and just then, he saw a small girl in the window pane. It was the scout, her eyes dancing. Then she was gone, her hair flipping against the glass as she darted away, and it all went black.

DREAD CREW 1st ANNUAL
JUNK 'N' JOY FESTIVAL

It's a hot dog party, there's no doubt—come dressed like
PIRATES and propriety FLOUT! We'll DANGLE from
the scuppers! We'll DANCE in the mud! We'll SWING
from the mainstay and gulp ROCKBEER from jugs!
Bring your wounded, your tired, all your best JUNK.
We'll consult on how to JIG up its FUNK. Bring your
ideas for a brainstormin' medley. For junk of all kinds,
the answer is DREADLY!
SATURDAY JULY 1
8 O'CLOCK IN THE MORNING UNTIL
WHENEVER YOU LEAVE
SPONAGLE HOLLOW, 13-GATE, ROUTE 4
NEW GERMANY, NOVA SCOTIA

The mysterious invitation spilled into the village, the town, the county, the province, and beyond. It was found stuffed between stacks at the village library, and stapled to telephone poles, and slid underneath plates at greasy spoons.

"I heard it's the same gang that trampled the flower show at Privateer's Wharf," the ladies' auxiliary gossiped at three o'clock tea. "And that smashed Gus Abato's dock and made off with three hundred—yes, Bess, three hundred—wheels of Gorgonzola, a verymost precious vintage, no less, straight off the boat from Italy!"

"Even the RCMP can't catch them, so vicious and wily they are, that's what Noreen's daughter said and she's a sergeant, and it's top secret, I'll have you know..."

"It would have to be actors, like at a theme park, wouldn't it? For real, actual pirates to have a real, actual pirate festival... unthinkable, isn't it?"

Suspicion turned to intrigue, just as Joe had hoped. Who could ignore such a proposition? The costume shop in Lunenburg couldn't keep black hats and dreadlock wigs and hoop earrings and eye patches and rag pants in stock, and thrift shops from Yarmouth to Cape Tormentine offered bins upon bins of disreputable rags for patching together.

Puzzled as they were, no one dared miss the spectacle.

"THUGS," Hector had bellowed one day at the beginning, arms outstretched, his crew leaning forward with anticipation. His voice filled every corner, every ear. "Be whipsmart or be gone. It's time to test your mettle, your trickery, your crookedness."

At the captain's back was a mountain of scrap metal, coils of frayed rope, battle-worn Styrofoam, moldy haystacks, a few salvaged army tents, and a selection of appliance parts and mechanical bits from Joe's hoard.

The crew surveyed the pile hungrily, muttering dibs.

"Team up," he ordered sternly. "Work in twos, and keep it secret. Think big. Think lineups. Think how to make them prissy folk stampede *to* us and not *from* us. Let's make this notion of Jackal's work—a pirate day for softies that gets us enough junk to get back in union black—and work like gangbusters. Got it? Now...GO!"

The crew fell upon the pile like sharks, plowing through the raw materials with the kind of decisiveness that only seasoned rejiggers possess. It had begun.

For a week of days and nights Joe's land rang with the almost constant din of hammering, sawing, cranking, and hoisting, each pirate worked near to the bone. What would be the fairgrounds—the old cornfield, the clearing by the pond, the meadow at the forest edge—now held mound after mound of mystery concealed with tents and tarps and guarded with watchful eyes.

Chapter Eleven

THE KICKER GETS IT GOING

"*Psst.*"

In the thick of midnight Eric fluttered one eye and sank into his quilt, lost in a dream more appealing than the prospect of being awake.

"Tracker."

He bolted up in bed to see the scout girl sitting on his windowsill, one leg dangling over the edge. *Please tell me I'm not wearing the crocodile pajamas.* Eric looked down (a plain t-shirt and long johns) and breathed out.

"It's you," he whispered.

"You been waitin'?" she grinned.

"Actually, yes," he replied, throwing back the blankets and reaching for his fleece. "I figured you're not the sort to break into houses for no good reason. I figured you'd be back."

"It's time to talk," she said, hopping off the sill and landing on the floor of his bedroom with a light thump. "You got any food?"

The house was long past asleep and in the pitch black the two crept like cats down the stairs to the kitchen, where the last embers of the wood stove cast an orange glow into the room. As

Missy settled onto a stool Eric brought bread and jam and milk to the trestle table, where they ate quietly for a while. Then she spoke.

"My name's Missy. I scouted you while you tracked us, and something told me you might be useful, and I'm here to tell you that as of tomorrow"—she looked at the clock—"or, today—you may as well be in on it with us, and with Joe."

"I already know Joe's got something to do with it." Eric choked back a faint bitterness at all that he'd shared with Joe, and at all that Joe had apparently not shared with him. "What I don't know is, why trust me? How do you know I won't call the Mounties?"

"Because you're like me," she said plainly. "You saw 'em and you reached out to hang on."

Missy spoke and Eric listened, and as the story unfolded Joe became something bigger in the mind of the boy, something much more than eccentric, and all was forgiven.

Perched on her daddy's shoulders, little Molly Robson began to squirm. Her clock was her belly, and her after-breakfast snack was at eight o'clock sharp every morning. The brass pocket watch of the ever-prompt Ms. Barrington, the schoolteacher, showed five past eight. She tapped the glass. So on and so on, a sudden awareness of the passing minutes rippled through the crowd.

Thousands of people—tens of thousands, it seemed—had descended from near and far. In a field along the edge of the crown forest, caravans, trailers, bike wagons, and backpacks piled high with junk stretched out as far as the eye could see, funnelling towards Joe's gate—children and dads and moms and nanas and grampas and all other sorts unrecognizable with the disrepute and filth of pirate dress.

They clamoured at the driveway fence as neatly as a mass of innately polite curiosity-seekers could clamour, peering for signs of life.

"What's the deal?"

"Can you see anything?"

"What're all these logs stuck upright for, all in a row? Look, someone's poured cement to put them there…"

"We've got the right day, right?"

"Hallooo, anyone here?"

They were respectable folk, despite all appearances. They'd expected a ticket booth, or a hand-stamper, or a FESTIVAL TODAY banner. Something Official. But the air was still, and not a sound could be heard but the rustling of the trees.

An old flagpole stood forlorn on the head of the fence post. Without warning a pulley kicked up a cloud of dust with a *SPROING!* The crowd gasped. Then, again: *CREEEEAK! CREEEEAK! CREEEEAK!* The rope joggled up by some invisible force as those at the front of the queue leapt back. It hit the top of the pole with a clang and the crowd hushed as the droop of fabric unfurled on the breeze—a skull and crossbones.

Buried among the bodies were two small figures that blended in the throng of pirate dress but shared between them nerves of a whole different breed.

"You're closer than you think…" Eric recalled Missy's parting taunt from the day they'd first met. *They've been next door all this time. I'm either the crummiest tracker ever born, or they're the sneakiest pirates.* People began to jostle as confusion spread and Missy gave Eric a nudge.

"It's got to be you," she said to him plainly as bodies around them shifted and bumped in panic.

"Me?" cried Eric. "To do what?"

"You be the kicker."

"The what?" he sputtered, exasperated.

"The kicker triggers the booby trap," she explained. "The kicker gets it all going."

A rush of what felt like honour spread up from the bottom of Eric's feet.

"You might as well," she smiled. "You've been chasin''em long enough. All I'll say is this—stay low. Real low."

Eric grasped her hand and gave it a squeeze, the grime and stickiness between her fingers leeching onto his. Then he dropped to all fours to weasel his way through legs and boots and wagon wheels to the front of the line.

Kneeling in the mud there was the youngest Pentz kid, Billie, staring at a bright red lever at the base of the fence post that had gone unnoticed by everyone else. Wrapping around it in sloppy paint were the words PULL ME and the girl turned to Eric boggle-eyed.

"Lookit!" she whispered, pointing at the obvious. "Lucas Cormier, he said they're real, and Jess Greene told him to shut it, but then Connor Pringle said they're real too, his crazy auntie told him so…"

She was beside herself.

Eric willed himself to look more authoritative than he felt. "In the story, the cup told Alice to DRINK ME and she did and the plate told Alice to EAT ME and she did and then all kinds of wonderful things happened. Right?"

Billie nodded solemnly, bolstered by cool-headed company. She then turned to sneak one hand between the knees of Father Jim, who wore pants of purple velvet, and grasped the lever tightly for a good, strong yank.

What happened next happened so fast, so suddenly, that no one had time to jump back. A wall of camouflaged netting and brush sprang up and enclosed the queue on its field side, and a band of performers (so they all thought) were catapulted into the air on zip-cables threaded between makeshift landing platforms and the tree canopy of the bordering forest.

"AIAIAIAIEEEEEE!" they all screeched in unison, waving legs and arms and whipping dreadlocks, soaring over the sea of people. Everyone shrieked and jumped.

"About time, you lot o' dough-for-brains! Good on you, girl!" shrieked Meena as she shot past upside down.

Beaming, Eric and the girl scrambled to their feet, she
pushing back through the mob to find her folk and he striding
forward purposefully towards the sprung-open gate. He sensed
that Missy was behind him and the two of them entered the
field, leaving behind them at the gate hundreds and thousands
of stunned people, struck by what they saw.

"Ho there, young whippersnap!" bellowed what looked like a
flying bear. "Ants in your pants, have yeh?"

The lady-pirate swooped to within a foot of Eric's head and
he shuddered, caught in the breeze of a nemesis—although his
gut told him in this case, ants-in-pants were deemed a mighty
fine thing.

"Nice moves, Gretch!" Missy called back. "Amos, watch that
rusty carabiner! I wouldn't flip like that or you'll smash up that
pretty nose o' yours…"

Eric turned as he walked to watch the hesitating crowd
and the pirate beasts that circled it. There was the gigantic
bearess who'd slingshotted herself back round, and an oafish
one that trailed the stink of a sulfur mill despite the open air.
There were a few skinny ones, each of them wiry like bats, and
a stout, bossy she-pirate with prickled greenery strapped to her
back. A beaming, corn-rowed fellow whirled back and forth
chirping *Right this way, folks, this way please!* and another had
combustible boosters strapped to his feet. With every gust of
wind he shot flames and lurched forward with a whoop.

Eric walked backwards now to take in the scene, the will of

his spyhood crumbling. He'd never seen such a sight. *Are they the bad guys? Am I the good? Whose side am I on now, and to what end?* He didn't know anymore, and didn't mind the not knowing.

"Look at you, grinnin' like a cat with a mouse," said Missy. "We've got to get there first, get rid of all the tarps. Let's go!"

As they raced headlong across the field ahead of the crowd, one voice amplified itself above the rest.

"Greetings, fellow rousers!" Sam bellowed into the megaphone, ushering the crowd forward from overhead. "Right this way fer hot dog day! I run the slimebucket of this gig. Sam's my name, if ya give a fig! Wha', yous all got gluesticks fer feet? Make tracks, mates! Make tracks!"

The first few bodies of the first few hundred shuffled forward. It was slow going, encumbered as they were with their wagons and backpacks and bikes—but pirate-pretender by pirate-pretender, excitement rippled through the crowd as the line began to move.

"This is even better than the dinner theatre in Summerside," declared Father Jim to no one in particular. "How very realistic they are, these actors! They even *smell* bad!"

From his perch in the branches of a nearby apple tree, Joe watched as countless people flooded the festival grounds. Every one of the pirates had been hooked up to Reggie's zip-cord slingshot, and they cackled and whooshed through the air as visitors streamed onto his land rolling carts and carrying blueprints under arms and pulling tractors and trailers loaded heavy with propositions and projects. It filled Joe fit to burst.

"Nobody'll come," Ewsula had muttered early that morning as the pirates clipped into the slingshot one by one.

"They will, Ewsie, you'll see," Joe had replied, smiling kindly even though he wasn't sure himself. He clicked her harness onto the wire and she sunk her head, unconvinced.

He'd turned to face the crew, strangely quiet. Reggie wore his best dribble bibble. Johnnie, covered in sawdust as usual, had carved himself an intricate wooden chestplate. Meena's head was so ruthlessly plucked that it shone an even more startling pink than usual. Ewsula, resplendent in all seventeen of her prized rat tail necklaces and a cape of long-haired yak fur, stood as still as a statue, sweating profusely and murmuring to herself. Phezzie had spent two hours before dawn rubbing rock salt under his arms and boiling his socks fruitlessly. Willie had promised to not blow anything up, and so wore a one-piece suit of stretchy black material (which did not allow for the concealment of explosives) to prove his good intentions. *That's funny*, thought Joe fleetingly. *I don't recall Will being quite so...tall...*

The dawn's mist had just begun to lift. Less than an hour, by Joe's reckoning, and they'd start seeing townspeople come over the west ridge towards the main gate. It was the biggest of days and the usually unflappable crew—even the captain, who had knotted his beard into submission—were shifty and restless.

They've been so busy invading and attacking, they've never welcomed—nor been welcomed, Joe had thought to himself. *Fish out of water, they are.*

"Don't worry," he'd said earnestly, looking at them in turn. His own face was painted in artful stripes of soot and seaweed paste, his solitary dreadlock wrangled neatly into a classic monkey's fist. "Just be yourselves."

Ike scratched his head contemplatively, and a faint rustling from his lapel told Joe that he'd dressed in his lucky cockroach-pocket sports coat.

"What I mean to say," he added pleadingly, "…is to be the verymost courteous sort of yourselves."

Reggie belched and the crew broke into chuckles.

"Right, you heard the man," said Hector. "I'm same as you today, just plain Dread. This day, Jackal's in charge." The crew nodded solemnly. "No kid-tossin', no pantsin', no bilge dunkin'. You figure out what honey means, and you be it. Got it?"

"Aye, sir," they'd saluted, clanking awkwardly, attached in a row to the zip-cord.

Eased by the familiar routine of orders, the nerves in the air had faded and the crew had forged ahead with final preparations as the sun rose in the sky.

And here they all were now, zipping overhead and trading friendly barbs with partygoers pouring onto the festival field. *We're in the swing of it now,* thought Joe, surveying all from his perch. *What a start to the day!*

Chapter Twelve

THE DAY THAT HONEY WON

Joe's land was churned up like melting chocolate, happily trampled. Townsfolk and pirates alike were in the mightiest of high spirits, shouting to one another and tossing tools and rope and mechanical bits hand-to-hand over the heads of the revellers. The air was filled with clanks and bongs as hammers struck home, as wrenches twisted and chains cranked. Rambunctious boys and girls weaved through the crowd trailing strips of ragged cloth, squealing and chasing. Every now and then as Joe wound his way through the field a hand slapped his back in affection, someone or another jostling him to say *Good on you, Joe! What a grand day!*

Shoulder to shoulder (or, truthfully, shoulder to elbow, Joe being so proper-sized and Hector being so pirate-sized), Jackal and the captain strolled through the grounds dodging piles of scrap wood and trailers of rope and buckets of paint and sponges and steel cable, the air buzzing with collaboration.

"Hey mistah!" chirped a voice as a small, sticky hand tugged the pantleg of the most wanted, most ruthless vagrant in the country.

Hector looked down his nose to where the girl stood, a study in giant and miniature. The girl's gangly, nervous companion—a big brother, perhaps—stood shaking like a leaf beside her, peering doubtfully from under the brim of his hat.

"Tweats!" exclaimed the child, holding up her fist and opening it reverently. "I-a sellin' tweats! A nickel fer two, two nickels fer three, three nickels fer..."

She rattled on proudly and Joe peered into her hand at a selection of linty, bright-green candies and dried up wads of bubblegum in torn foil wrappers, squashed with age. For a moment they stood frozen in gesture—the girl smiling widely with no fear of harm, and Hector looking down at her speechless because of it.

"I'll take the lot," the captain's voice cracked as he spoke. "That'll be five—no, six loonies at least, and don't you settle for a penny less. And I'll tell you what else, young vagabond. It just so happens I'm short one sweetsmaster on my ship, the last one, you know, he was stole off by our cousin locomotive crew the Blitzriders of the London Underground, they go crazy for licorice allsorts, you know, they can't get enough an' we been short-handed ever since..."

As he walked away, the sprite propped on his shoulder and her big brother scrambling along behind, the captain turned back to Joe with a look of great fulfillment. Just then had been the first time anyone had ever been friendly to Hector Gristle. Not because he was boss. Not because he would string you up. Not because he was about to have you goop-shot. But just because.

Joe watched the new twosome bob away through the crowd, smiling to himself. *Everything's going to change, it really is, and for everybody.*

"VIOLATORS!" a screech pierced the air and in the startled silence that followed came the hissing of cats. Bertha Pringle's outrage had forced a clearing and the captain, sensing an answering-to, knelt discreetly to release the would-be sweetsmaster and her brother to the sheltering anonymity of the crowd. With one arm raised to accost the leader of the dreaded Dreads the woman shrieked, "CRIMINAL! VAGRANT! Rats, the lot of you—no-good, stinking RATS!"

In high shanty style, the ever-defiant Bertha wore a girdle of impenetrable beige overtop coveralls of hunting orange, her cats a seething mass that snaked in figure eights round her ankles.

"We meet again, madam," Hector's voice rang out as Amos and Ike moved instinctively to his side. "Though the last time we did, rats were deemed a juicy treat, were they not?"

"BOSH!" she cried, flailing furiously as crew within earshot abandoned fairground posts to collect themselves for this most curious standoff.

Meena, the smallest of all the lady-pirates save lung capacity, stepped forward with an uncommonly gentle air and the madwoman paused, panting, her eyes bulging.

"Clever garb, that is." Meena circled the incensed woman.

"Me long johns are ferever sneakin' down round m'knees, 'specially when I'm runnin', but undies on the outside…that's a fine trick. Makes yeh feel all-tucked-in, eh?"

The woman they called lunatic turned a brighter shade of pink.

"Y-y-you…CRETINS!" she screeched. "Roughed up my shanty, you did! Upset my kitties!"

As Bertha's tirade continued, more Dreads quietly found their way to Hector's side, and Joe leaned across Frankie to Vince. "Please tell me you didn't give Bertha Pringle a hard go of it, Vince. She's got her own way of seeing things…"

The first mate shuffled defensively.

"We went down there jus' before we came upon you, and Phezzie near-about lost his head for all the old railway spikes, and we was jus' loadin' up when we seen her place crawlin' like an anthill with cats, and so we had to take 'er fer all she had…"

Joe frowned.

"It was the litter—kitty litter," Vince continued. "It's the most abrasive stuff we can get our hands on, and sure enough she had cartons full of it. Fer deck tack, and fer Phezzie's socks, and to scrub out the vat when it needs a swish…"

Meanwhile, Bertha was unstoppable.

"I t-t-tried to warn these…" (she gestured at the crowd) "… these IMBECILES, but they say 'She's nutters!' and now look at them, cavorting with y-y-you…VULTURES!"

Through the press of bodies the slight figure of Willie entered Bertha's circle and she turned to him, her cats following suit, and they stared at one another until Willie spoke, the boosters in the soles of his feet leaking tendrils of smoke.

"Yer jus' like ma mam," he murmured too softly to be heard by anyone but her. "Ma mam, she used to rave jus' like you. She never 'ad nobody to listen, and so she never got no calm."

"R-r-roughnecks…" she murmured, but the steam of her rage was dissipating.

"You's a good 'nuff lady. Look at yeh wit' yer *bebittes,* 'ow dey love yeh so. Dat's not crazy miss, *non. Comment dit-on…*" He searched the air, then raised one finger as he found the word he sought. "*Ah, oui. Ca c'est* nobility."

Steeled as she was to mockery and contempt, the lunatic woman blinked, her eyes glistening.

"No one else cares for 'em but me." Her cats matched her growing ease, retracting claws. "They come all up in me nooks and me crannies and they keep me warm, an' so I return the favour is all."

Willie nodded. "Ma mam, she was right about a whole lotta thing. It's jus', not 'nuff folk are *confortable* wit' a bit o' crazy. We are. *Ben oui,* we call it spunk."

After a long pause she spoke haltingly.

"You… you coulda jus' asked me an' my boys and girls where we gets our litters, so as you'd get some fer yerselves."

Hector moved forward to join Willie. "Fair enough," he raised his voice as well as both arms to demand the attention of all, as was his vocation. "Let it be marked that on this day, the

Dread Crew issues its first formal apology, and let it be to this fine woman and her wee fiends, for we are in her debt."

The bulk of the crew had assembled round the edges of Bertha's wrath and together they saluted and sank to knees and bowed, each offering a nod of regret in whatever manner felt most fitting.

Amid the cheers could be made out cries of "'Atta girl, Bertha!" and "You showed 'em, Knickers!" and it wasn't just the acknowledgement of a band of merciless thugs that had Bertha Pringle feeling heard for the first time in her life. It was the high-fives of her neighbours, her fellow citizens, her kin.

The perimeter of the grounds were strung with garlands of moss and pinecone, with log benches for folk to rest with a rockbeer and take in the midsummer air. Here is where Joe sat for a while to survey the day, his feet crossed at the ankles.

He saw a lineup at the Inventions Tent and a crowd spilling out of Tinkerer's Alley, a dead-end stretch of logging road lined with workbenches manned by restoration specialists and jury-riggers.

Zeke leapt around the edges of his All-You-Can-Eat Hot Dog Fire Pit, barking at his stick-turning brutes as red-hot coals sent clouds of fragrant smoke into the air. "HUP! HUP!" he waved his arms, his stir-stick swinging as always from the rope at his waist. "TWO! STICK TWO HUP!" Amos and Ike perched high above the sparks on heatproof stilts, passing steaming sticks with dozens of hot dogs pierced on each to hearty applause at the canteen.

Ewsula and Gretch's Haunted Forest Moss Maze looked like an ant farm for all the adventurers inside it, and no wonder—it was an intricate web of tunnels, trick dead ends, and booby traps with translucent walls of slick-wet kelp, mottled bark ceilings, and curtains of stretched moss. A sign at the entrance read PHIND THE PHUNK, YOUR NOSE KNOWS. Anyone able to uncover Phezzie won the prize of a plug-nosed shoulder ride or malt cider tickets, depending on the size and inclination of the finder—but the blanketing effect of Phezzie's odour made him impossible to pinpoint within a fifty-foot radius. Joe watched as a group of women wearing matching "Mayflower Handquilters' Society" ruffled shirts and floppy hats staggered out the other side amid gales of laughter—unsuccessful, they'd been, and they were soaked to the skin with slime and good humour.

Sam's Dirt Luge track careened down the slope above the pond, with mini-Barrows that exploded through hollow speedbumps made of finely crusted mud. Racers splashed at a high velocity into the sludge and weeds at the finish line, drenched and entangled in pond scum and lily pads, only to scramble, trip, and giggle their way back up to the starting gate.

Brimming with satisfaction, Joe rose to join Johnnie, Willie, and Reggie at the starting gate of their Booby Trap Gang Run. Polite folk crawled and climbed and yelped and stomped through the obstacle course, their friends on the sidelines hooting and cheering, while the three pirates stood proud with hands on hips.

"A mastery o' wood engineerin'," Johnnie beamed. Reggie responded with a snicker, more pleased with himself for adding the spring-loaded anthill jump.

"I'll eat *mon* pant if anyone gets past my smokin' pommel 'orse," added Will. "*Un testament* o' trickery, *bien sûr*. Come t'ink of it, *c'est le* 'ole flippin' day."

"Go," Missy nudged Eric and sank back into the crowd, promoting him by way of abandonment. He stood at the table's edge, frozen.

The pirate wore a black apron and a distinctive head scarf, and was bent over an antique motor dwarfing everything he touched. "Blast you," he hissed. "Do as yeh should."

He pulled the choke and yanked on the starter and the feeble thing coughed, but that was all. The small crowd that had formed chuckled, not remotely disappointed.

"Ahh, see, this relic's more a relic than the relic tryin' to fix it, eh?" The onlookers chuckled their agreement and as the first mate looked up to address the engine's owner, his eyes fell on the slight boy who stood before him—the very same boy he'd seen skulking and restless, daring to poke around the edges of his crew's trail.

"And you, kid. Care to have a go?" Vince fixed his gaze onto Eric with an equal measure of amusement and opposition. *I know who you are.*

The inside of Eric's mouth felt like Velcro. For a long time he stood there blank as the imposing figure stared intently, a wink on his face and...was that...maggots? Maggots *in his beard?*

"I...I...don't..."

I am a hunter. He took a breath and tried again.

"It's the crank, I think."

The pirate raised one eyebrow, and Eric stepped forward.

"You've got to hold the intake valve in one hand and crank the engine in the other at the same time, and then you let go of the valve, and then it should start since then you're not working against compression. There's a chance it might fire and kick back at you, but at least it'll start."

Vince nodded and backed away from the table, gesturing for Eric to continue. Streams of people filed through the greenway for tinkerers, casting friendly glances at the unlikely collaborators as they passed.

"My dad's got one just like this in our old tractor. It's finicky and puts you off at first but all you need is to figure out how it likes things to be."

Enlivened, the engine's owner bent happily over her charge, followed Eric's direction, and brought the engine sputtering to life to a chorus of enthusiastic clapping. Vince leaned over the table after an approving pause.

"Well put, kid, well put." He offered his hand for Eric to shake by way of introduction. "Reminds me of a few buddies of mine, eh?"

He smiled and Eric smiled back, up to his nose.

Some time later, Joe hopped up on an overturned crate to peer
over the heads of the crowd and saw Sam already watching for his
signal, eyes bright. Joe nodded imperceptibly as the two had dis-
cussed. The time had come. The gunner wove through the crowd
slick as an eel, the only one of the crew who'd been made privy
to Joe's biggest inventive coup—the vinegar-to-honey rejigging
of Sam's beloved Gooperator. He'd been waiting weeks for this.

Anchored at the southwest corner of the field among
the brambles, the Barrow appeared as nothing more than a
ramshackle old barn. Unaware of the existence of such a thing
as pirate woodships and gloriously distracted by the festivities,
the townsfolk had failed to notice the ship's cogs, its wheels, the
lines encircling the pilot's perch high above, its distinctly un-
barnlike silhouette and mounting ladders.

"Get a load o' that." Gretch nudged Joe, watching from a
distance as Leonard, the city librarian, leaned unknowingly
against the gangplank to pick a rock out of his boot. "It's like a
starvin' grizzly bear hidin' out at a tea party."

None afforded this nondescript bulk more than a passing
glance. For if they had, they would have sensed it was almost
alive, leaning into the wind, taut like a wild dog on a too-short
chain. And they would have been afraid.

So when Sam gave the crankshaft a pop-kick and the engine
backfired and coughed a cloud of smoke into the air (Joe

frowned, puzzled—*That'll need a look-at...*), thousands of faces swung around to gawk at the sight. The grizzly had awakened.

Many among the outer edges of the crowd fled towards the woods (*Unwise*, thought Joe, remembering the swath the Barrow once cut through tree and rock and earth) but then they crept back, overcome with curiosity, forming a spontaneous grass road edged with spectators. They pointed and shouted in awe, now accustomed to the rumbling (indeed, a much dampened, more friendly rumble to what it once had been) and smoke and sputtering.

"ATTENTION!" yelled Sam redundantly into the megaphone he'd procured for this very moment.

(One week earlier, hair slicked to the scalp and face scrubbed till his pockmarks shone, he'd dressed in Joe's only suit and ventured to the junior high school in search of the soccer coach, who was rumoured to have a voice-amplifying device. Out of his usual rags Sam looked a sort of strange you couldn't put your finger on, but when he approached the man and asked him haltingly to let him borrow the thing for work at Joe's homestead, the man had simply handed it over, smiling. *Just drop it off at the locker room when you're done*, the man had said. *And pass on our hellos to Joe, will you?* It befuddled Sam deeply that forcible worm-gargling had not been required for him to get what he wanted.)

"PIRATE BOYS AND PIRATE GIRLS, 'SPECIALLY MUCKY ONES, FOLLOW THIS HERE VESSEL IF

YOU WANT SOMETHIN' TO TICKLE YER TONGUE.
NO GROWN-UPS! NO COOTS! NO KROTCHY OLD
STIFFS! STEP IN LINE FOR A SWEET THAT'S FINE."

He dropped the megaphone on the planks of the deck with a
clatter and eased the Barrow forward at a crawl.

Follow? Poppy Weston stood bright-eyed at the edge of the
crowd. *Us on foot, follow that thing? It'll swallow us whole!* and
after a flicker of consideration she decided *Cool!* and scrambled
to just out of range of the rear exhaust, still close enough to see
splinters. More joined her, hundreds it seemed, girls and boys
in flounces and velvet smeared with mud, picking their way
across the great ruts crushed into the earth by the Barrow's
wheels.

Finally the woodship came to a halt in the centre of the
festival grounds, and with one last sputtering belch, the engine
went quiet. Sam popped his head over the edge of the pilot's
perch to see a gathering of curious, tiny people far below, and a
throng of moms, dads, and onlookers hovering in the distance.

"Right there, mates," he yelled, scrambling to the turret and
fiddling with something the children couldn't see. "Back up,
now, back up…that's it…farther…a little more…"

The sun had blazed down all day, and by now pretenders
and scoundrels alike were tugging uncomfortably at clothes.
Poppy took in the ship high above, the muck underfoot, and the
waiting boys and girls, flushed and stifled. Impatient, she cupped
her hands over her mouth.

"What now?" she inquired, standing as tall as she could. "You said sweets!"

"Sweets?" Sam taunted from the perch, wiping a most fitting smudge of grease off his forehead. "Did somebody want SWEETS?"

Before any of the upturned faces had time to react a great belch erupted from the guts of the beastly ship and then SPLOOOOOOOSHHHHH!

Glorious and icy-cool, the reformed Gooperator spewed wave after wave of blackberry slush over the mini-pirate mob. Sam whooped and hollered at the trigger as purple-drenched kids giggled and squealed and scattered like ants.

"They'll be stained from top to tail for two weeks," exclaimed Ms. Barrington as the dripping, sticky, finger-licking crew came stumbling back towards the grown-ups, the refurbished Barrow purring contentedly in the thick of it all. The old teacher shook her head with a smile, casting aside her customary sternness, grateful for the air's new and misty tartness.

As the day went on the pirates mingled beautifully, in high demand not only for shoulder rides and mock monster chasing but to consult in huddles of invention. Zeke's stilt-aided lava pit had inspired the local firefighters so much, he'd been asked to lead a how-to workshop for their barbeque fundraisers—and they'd offered heatproof boots in return. Ewsula and Gretchen would be brought specially into the city for a meeting with the curator of the Nova Scotia Museum, who had been through their moss maze and wanted their minds set to a new diorama exhibit of ancient forests. And Willie, entranced with the marching band from the naval base in Halifax (who had turned up to perform in full pirate regalia), had turned bright pink with pride when the major approached him and said, "Come and be our timpani-banger!" Already the pirate had dreamed up drumsticks that would shoot sparks.

Joe strode through the grounds and weaved in and out of conversations, greatly satisfied. *Folk and fiends side-by-side, sparking friendships and odd jobs and usefulness amongst themselves...this day is everything and more.*

The universe, apparently eagle-eyed for jinxes on that day, took note.

Chapter Thirteen

SIRENS OF RECKONING

As referee for the obstacle course, Missy's perch afforded her a bird's-eye view. She sat cross-legged atop a refurbished lifeguard station level to the top of the climbing wall, scanning the crowd. A stream of revellers and a festive glow spilled out from between the canvas flaps of the army tent, which housed a raucous band (she could tell that well enough, watching them sweat) and the thumping of hundreds of feet. Across the fairgrounds folk lingered and laughed and traded ideas and inventions, handing tools to one another overhead, swapping skills and brainstorming. Behind the barns, so as not to take up valuable people-space, lay honey's prize—a pile of junk big enough for a year's worth of drops. There was a flurry of movement and Missy smiled as a gang of kids found Phezzie and tackled him to the ground, all of them plugging their noses in disgust and swooning uproariously.

It was all meant to be this way, she thought to herself, grinning as Amos slicked his hair back to sign the autograph book of three giggling teenagers far below. *It was meant for me to find them and for them to find me, and this right here is just exactly where I'm to be.*

At this very moment, as she reflected on good fortune and fate and luck, goosebumps rose. Through crowd and trees she caught a flash of industrial white rolling down the dirt road towards the main gate.

"No, no, no!" The unshockable girl scrambled down and landed in a heap, then ran through the field bouncing off oblivious bodies like a pinball towards the ship—for the captain, for Vince, for whatever chance was left for warning and evasion.

A cheerful face cut through her panic—it was the tracker, Eric. He waved at her and she shook her head, her face frenzied, tugging at his shirt as she passed.

"What the...what's wrong?!" he struggled to match her pace as she weaved through a wall of people and carts, hurdling over crates and tools and piles. She reared up on the Barrow's splintered hull and leapt upon it, climbing catlike up the chain net until she disappeared up and over the lip of the deck. He followed, swinging one leg over the edge, and then the other.

I've just climbed aboard a pirate ship. THE pirate ship...

"Snap out of it!" She shook him. "Look at me, tracker, and listen. We've got to do a rolling kickstart. Loosen that rope while I..."

The wail of a siren interrupted, long and shrill, loud enough to register through even her dampened ears, lighting her face on fire.

"Hurry!" she cried. As more sirens wailed he did as he was told, which was no easy task, neither of them being the proper height. Jumping and climbing up they wound wheels and slopped grease on metal parts and loosened cables, a seemingly unending ritual of tasks necessary to ready the ship.

"They been careless, stayed too long in one place," she spoke breathlessly, cranking pistons into place by hand. "They haven't been to the depot in three months. Blast it, I shoulda said somethin'…"

"Depot? What depot? What's going on, Missy?" yelled Eric, his hands over his ears.

"The union depot," she yelled at him over the rising wail of sirens, exasperated, throwing him one end of a ground-mooring rope. "They're in deep dirt now, and there's no time to explain, now uncleat that and PULL!"

As Joe watched the crowd jostle happily at the flap of the tent, his fulfillment was broken by the sharp wail of a siren. Folk dropped armfuls and reached out to grab the scruffs of beloved children and draw them close. Another siren joined in, then another, and another until ear-splitting wrongness came from everywhere all at once.

The only figures among the crowd not frozen in puzzlement were the crew. Amos and Ike, the stumps of their stilts still red-hot and burning, lumbered like stick insects out of the fire pit and across the field towards the Barrow, sprinting in slow motion with unbendable ten-foot legs. Zeke exploded out from behind the canteen, knocking the whole thing over with a crash.

Scrambling in the swath cleared by his stilted brutes he cupped
his hands over his mouth and bellowed "CODE B! CODE B!
ALL DREADS TO SHIP!"

From the obstacle course at the farthest end of the field
Reggie, Ike, and Johnnie plowed faster than anyone would
have expected of such giants, waving their arms and roaring
MOOOVE! at the stunned crowd. Others joined—Phezzie and
Ewsula and then Gretch and Vince—until the whole crew was
a sprinting mob that throbbed with a tangle of pounding limbs
and dreadlocks and trailed a breeze of filth and shrieks, the
captain's tree-trunk legs shaking the ground at the lead.

Then the sirens stopped. Hector slowed. The others piled up
at his back and, panting, they turned slowly towards what would
be the second invasion of Joe's land this season—this time an
unassuming row of white cube vans that rolled through the gate
and up the road towards the crowd, each one sporting an air
horn on the front grill, now unnecessary.

"If yeh hear the sirens…" panted Johnnie through a haze of
his own sawdust, "…it's too late."

Heaving with exertion the others either simply collapsed
or stood with hands on knees, adopting a defeated stance as
the crowd parted in familiar obedience to what was, to them,
authority.

"Take me to the captain," the woman ordered briskly to the
first person she encountered upon disembarking from the

vans—Joe, who had manoeuvred so. She wore an outfit not unlike that of a school principle, impeccably tidy with sturdy black boots and a sheath of sensible beige, her hair pinned into tight submission. She was strangely disarming though, more efficient than sinister, and handed her card to Joe. It said simply *Chief, T.H.U.G.S.S.*

Joe hesitated but, like the others, was more inclined to cooperate than to provoke.

"Right this way, ma'am," he said softly. He led her to Hector, stepping back respectfully as the two locked eyes.

"Captain Gristle," she said curtly.

"Chief," the giant nodded.

She turned to scan the crowd and the remnants of the festivities, one eyebrow raised. *Hector's not the only one with a flair for performance,* Joe thought.

"You have broken cover," she said simply.

"It would seem so," the captain was expressionless.

"You have diverted union food allowance."

"Indeed we have," he agreed. She narrowed her eyes and sighed decisively.

"You play at nonchalance, Captain, and so I will not mince words. This crew has shown a continued deficit, and junk remittance as well as mobility have been unsatisfactory for three quarters in a row. The sentence will be doubled, of course, for continued evasive tactics, and our discoveries here today will naturally be factored in to the determination of punitive action."

The shamed stance of the pirates turned to sputtering, gaping disbelief.

"The distraction witnessed here today warrants a citation of Pointlessness, which is a capital offence," she continued, her voice brisk with the surety of rules and the breaking of them. "Indeed, it is one of this organization's most severe charges. This crew has loitered, wilfully unengaged in sanctioned rampage—not to mention the irreparable breach of security caused by such a public display as this. This crew will now face the consequences."

With hushed urgency, word spread through the crowd that unknown enforcers had condemned the most fabulous day the province had ever seen. Drenched in muck and violet slush, with wigs and scarves askew, a wall of pirate pretenders closed in on the scene, abandoning projects and tools and diversions to step forward, to witness.

"This crew will be taken to headquarters immediately to begin their sentence of two years' housetoil effective immediately," the chief announced loudly, unfazed. "Their ship will be confiscated and reassigned to one of three probationary crews on the shortlist. That is all."

The crowd exploded into an uproar of protest, booing and hissing as the Reds moved to corral the pirates into the vans to be taken away.

Eric raised the last groundrope arm over arm. As it thumped

over the rail it released a cloud of the same dried mud that had settled over every artifact of his spyhood, starting with his prize discovery—the rulebook of the Dreads' apparent doom. And here he was a part of it—thrills!—a player in the scheme to rescue foes that might instead be friends. He was yanked like the rope into the sudden realization that the contribution he'd make was exactly what he'd been meant for—not to catch but to save.

"We won't get far," Missy despaired, her face pressed against the porthole as she cranked the last piston furiously. "Without those brutes we'll never get her goin' fast enough to outrun the Reds, but we've got to try…"

Eric let the uncleated rope slip to his feet and took the girl by the shoulders, imploring her to listen in her way, and listen good.

"Missy," he said firmly. "I have an idea, but you're going to have to trust me."

The spark in him, so like her own, restored the girl. Her eyes narrowed and she nodded.

"We hide. We let them be taken." The words spilled out in a rush. "You're right—with just the two of us, we can't break through that convoy. Once the fair breaks up we'll bury it deeper in the woods so in case the union comes back, it's away from Joe's cabin. We've got to keep the ship safe, Missy, until they're out. I don't need to be a pirate to know there's no such thing as a captain without a ship."

Torn, she turned from his face to the standoff at the gate, first frantic and then resolved to what she knew was their only choice.

"The hillbrake…" Her voice trembled, but she met his eye, resolved. "It'll need the both of us."

With the engine still idling out of gear, Eric and Missy gripped four fists around the lever, jammed good and tight, and hauled. With a creak it gave loose and the hulk rolled silently backwards, tucking itself into further concealment in the brush behind Joe's cabin, now camouflaged as a shed, perhaps a barn. To the untrained eye the Barrow was certainly nothing of any consequence, although being inconsequential was against its nature, as it was a proud ship.

And so, counter to instinct, both the ship and the pirate-girl crouched fitfully, repressing the urge to crash through to their keepers.

Disciplinary officers reached for handcuffs as Chief B issued an order into her radio. "Confiscation crew—seize the ship."

Coveralled machinists wearing tool belts and helmets with face shields jumped out of a supply van and convened in front of the chief with almost a collective saunter, as the helm-taking of an empty ship was most often an uneventful task.

"Ready for duty, Chief," the team-lead addressed her. "But we scoped out the place as we drove in, and there's no ship to be seen."

The chief blinked incomprehensibly and turned to Hector, her eyes narrowing.

"There's no ship here and no ship nowhere," he said simply. "Scuttled."

A tension rippled from one pirate to the next and they all leaned in slightly, adopting the posture of the lie.

"Smashed her up past repair in attack on this very land. Burned what was left."

"Is that so?" She pursed her lips together with skepticism and studied the pirate captain in front of her. Sam shouldered past the guards to face the chief.

"Yeh knows us, yeh do!" the gunner was insolent. "All these prissy folk prancin' around thinkin' they's one of us? Playin' at bein' tough? Yeh think we'd sit here eatin' dogs all day and not hear a whisp of our Barrow?"

She hesitated.

"Why if our grand ship were wif' us now (Sam sniffed as if choking back angry tears, and the captain stifled a smirk)…we'd carve a path through this crowd o' Sunday drivers like a combine through hay."

Sam twisted his face into wickedness as Ike tilted back his head and roared to the sky, in mourning for what was apparently a lost ship. The rest of the crew nodded and growled, all of them now tapped into the melodrama.

The chief raised one arm into the air, signalling for silence. Despite the electricity of thousands of witnesses, Joe's land was as peaceful as a kitten's purr. There was a breeze, and the swish of poplar leaves, the call of crows, the shuffling of feet. After what felt like a long time the chief nodded, satisfied. For a rampaging woodship—that stinking, smoking, rumbling hulk as she remembered it, repulsive but effective—couldn't possibly exist in the midst of such unruffled peace.

"When did this...incident...occur?" She was all business now, ordinary in size except for when she spoke, and Joe marvelled at the charisma of her authority.

"Two months back, maybe more," Hector replied coolly, his eyes intent on hers.

"That makes this entire crew derelict of duty," she snapped. "You failed to submit the appropriate incident reports. You did not return to headquarters for reassignment. You...are... *dodgers*."

The crowd within earshot whispered, agitated, and she went on to answer the question already forming in Joe's head.

"Dodging plus your history of being under quota, Dreads, makes for a double sentence. That sentence starts now."

In the uproar and crush of officers Hector grasped Joe by the shoulders to whisper roughly in his ear.

"At this rate we's lookin' at years, Joe..." Joe startled at this first use of his everyday name. "Guard the junk we got today. We'll need it when we's out. It's not legit unless we drop it proper at a depot—if they see it now they'll claim it off our record, or worse they'll think we been settin' to keep it fer

ourselves. The ship…" the pace of his message quickened. "Put
her out o' sight. Keep 'er greased, take 'er round whenever it's
dark so the cogs don't seize. The wheels need to be ground down
every few months or else the cracks spread. We lost a wheelcap
a couple months back from goin' too long between grindin's and
it just about made her roll…had to get the ship winch-tugged
outta that one…"

The captain's face was pained as he was pulled away, corralled
into the vans with the others. On each of their faces Joe saw the
very same ache and worry—not so much a fear for their own
fate but a despair at being parted from their beloved ship.

Inside van three, Ironbound Ike stared straight ahead, wordless
as always. Meena, who sat opposite him, was uncharacteristically
silent as well, overcome. In the back of van eight, Zeke snapped
at the nervous chatter of Amos. Gretchen and Johnnie sat in
van two knee-to-knee, whispering solemnly. And so it was as
the contingent of transport vehicles idled, an array of nerves and
hushed fear.

From van one a female voice rang out across the radio.

"Union, fall out!" She was chipper, buoyed by a job well done.
"Return to headquarters."

The vans lurched ahead a few feet but then stopped. The
pirates turned to peer through windows and the voice rang out
again, this time amplified through the megaphone mounted on
the front grill of the chief's vehicle.

"Let us pass, or face charges of obstruction of justice," she called firmly.

Hector cleared his line of sight over the driver's shoulder and his jaw dropped. The wall of ordinary folk had closed in to form a human barrier, arms folded across chests.

"The people...they're blockin' the way," he murmured.

"They're...what?" cried Vince, who shared the captain's van. He leaned forward as the same realization rippled through to the rest of the crew, two by two, and like all the rest, Vince peered through the windshield at his first view of friendship from ordinary folk.

The voice of Chief B rang out once more.

"These scrappers are in violation of code and face a sentence of housetoil," she declared to the crowd. "Do not involve yourselves with what you do not understand."

A lone voice called out in response. It was Eric's father, who stood next to Joe.

"We understand plenty for now, if you don't mind me saying so," he said calmly. The crowd shuffled and nodded behind him, continually growing. "You carry with you friends of our Joe, and that makes them our friends, too."

Chief B glared through the windshield. Citizens intervening on behalf of pirates? It was unheard of. It was counter to generations of profitable scrapping.

"Not only that, but you've gone and deemed this day a waste of time," Eric's father continued. "We respectfully disagree."

On her orders the chief's van rolled to the edge of the crowd where Eric's father stood.

"You may submit appeals through the proper channels in the case of this crew's deliquency. We are founded upon order, efficiency, and due process. You are welcome to take advantage of it."

Through the window she offered a card to Eric's father, who'd been thrust into the role of impromptu spokesman. He glanced at it and handed it to Joe, who tucked it into his shirt pocket with a sigh.

"Back up, folks, back up," he called.

The crowd parted. As the vehicles rolled down the lane some townsfolk waved hesitantly, some shouted encouragement, and some scolded the authority—for what of this unforgettable day (and the strange, giant folk who pulled it all off) could be construed as wrong? The pirates, who had never been on the receiving end of friendship aside from that of one another, stared through the windows glassy-eyed and speechless.

The vans turned onto the main road and Zeke watched out the back window, the blur of well-wishers growing more distant.

"We's caught, our ship in hidin'." He slouched against the wall of the van. "An' I'm sittin' here smilin'. What happened here today…there's jus' no word fer that."

"Yes there is," mumured Amos. "The word fer that's *honey*."

Zeke nodded, for that was just it.

The sky was a watercolour, and the ground was littered with muddy footprints, trailer tracks, and stray ribbons. Throughout the field crows and gulls pecked diligently at forsaken hot dog buns, the only signs of life where there had been thousands only a couple of hours before.

From the helm, the tracker and the scout were silent, and the ship moved solemnly beneath their feet as though aware of its own refugee status. As dusk settled over the fairgrounds—now emptied of bewildered people, who had been ushered back to their homes after the union bust-up—Eric and Missy eased the Barrow to the shelter of the nearby forest. Eric placed a hand on the girl's shoulder and she turned to him with heavy eyes.

"We did the right thing," he said firmly. The ship lurched as its wheels pressed one last track into the meadow, leaving the grass for the roots and stones of the logging road.

Missy said nothing, disinclined as she was to fussy displays. After a pause, she spoke.

"Doing right doesn't make for feeling right," she said, to which there was no reply.

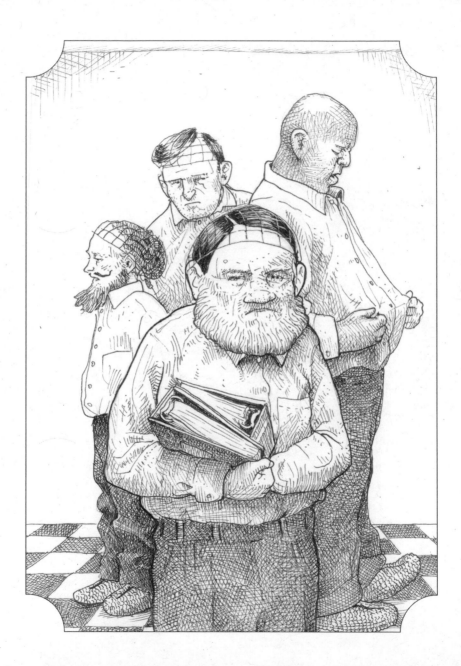

Chapter Fourteen

TOIL AND TROUBLE

NO ADMITTANCE BEYOND THIS POINT

HARD HATS AND STEEL TOES
REQUIRED ON PLATFORM

CAUTION: CHEMICALS, EXPLOSIVES,
BIO-HAZARDS

The convoy sped through a series of gates, a maze of chain-link fencing, and a menacing array of KEEP OUT signs and security checkpoints. T.H.U.G.G.S. union headquarters was an enormous box of corrugated steel at the end of the industrial peninsula, beyond the railway and dockyards of the city's downtown. It was trafficked by nobody, or at least nobody ordinary, and recognized at a distance by a very few as a nameless factory of no consequence.

But a great consequence it was—for pirates. It was the eastern seaboard home base, a fortification both relied upon and feared by shadow-ships of midnight. It was here that captains, brutes, engineers, and slimebuckets of all persuasions replenished supply stocks, reported for inspections, and dropped loads of junk on the depot platform by way of land, rail, sky, and sea. And then they faced reckonings in the form of either payment or prison.

"Pirates forward, please."

The crew unfolded themselves from the vans to assemble on the admissions deck, where a team in waterproof suits approached, led by a small man with a clipboard.

"Welcome, welcome!" He was oddly cheerful. "Before you begin your housetoil you must be processed, and I do apologize, but Chief's a stickler. Please remove all belongings down to your johnnies and place them in the provided bins for safekeeping. We—well, that means you (he gestured solicitously)—will then proceed to the scrubroom, where you will be made presentable for this facility. The room will be sealed, and then you will have thirty seconds to prepare yourself for the scrub cycle. Any questions?"

Someone sighed, but that was all.

"Right then! Let's get started, shall we? Pirates, this way please."

The crew was ushered into what resembled a car wash more than a shower, with a ceiling and walls full of sprinklers, hoses, and retractable brushes, and a floor spotted with a series of drains. As the crew began the process of shedding layers, the processing team turned to file out of the room. Behind them the door was shut with a clang, leaving the Dreads a filthy huddle in the centre of a sparkling void.

"Mrruggh." Ike voiced all there was to be said.

THWUCK! THWUCK! THWUCK! Without warning a barrel shot a volley of rubber ducks one after the other, each stamped PSYCHOLOGICAL AID, through a hole in the ceiling. The barrage continued for a few seconds, the room peppered with the sounds of an airgun and squeaking plastic that ricocheted off heads and landed onto the floor in a blast radius outside the huddle.

Phezzie snorted under his breath, nudging an offered duck with one of three bruised toes on his right foot. "I'll take your scrub cycle and raise you two compost heaps."

"I'll take ycr soap and raise you a faceful o' Gorgonzola," grumbled Zeke, his fist raised to the locked door.

"I'll take yer daisy-fresh and raise you a dungball," Reggie belched. Then he farted, a high-pitched sort of trumpety phoot, and outrage turned to snickering.

"Eww, eww, and ick all over, PIRATE COOTIES!" screeched Amos in falsetto, prancing on tiptoe, popping his eyes out and plugging his nose between finger and thumb. "Horrors and mores and I fear I might faint!"

By now the crew were in hysterics, pointing at one another's drooping underwear, tossing ducks, pinching each other's behinds, and feigning disgust at armpits. One enthusiastic nudge from Ike sent Phezzie's legs out from under him and

as he went down he yanked the leg of Ike's long johns, and
Ike reached out for the closest anchoring thing, which was
Ewsula's rat tails, and Ewsula yeowled and grabbed a fistful of
Willie's moustache, and they all slipped, landing in a tangled
pile on the floor just as a long beep emitted from a loudspeaker
in the corner. *ENJOY! YOUR. CLEANLINESS!* an automated
voice chirped, the advance of soap-infused jets of water that
pummelled the pirates from all directions.

It was instant mayhem. They tussled and howled, outraged
at first but then swept up in the ridiculousness of it all. Filth
encrusted into matted hair came off in globs, clogging the
drains, and the floor backed up, slick and swirling. The critters,
even less inclined to enjoy cleanliness than their host pirates,
skittered out in widespread panic. As Vince's maggots lost
their grip on his sopping beard they were squashed into jelly
underfoot, and a swarm of hissing cockroaches scuttled out from
Zeke's sopping johnnie pockets for dry footing.

The water ran from black to brown to green to clear, or
almost clear. The valves stopped, the door unsealed, and the
scrubmaster entered.

"That was a triple cycle with extra disinfectant…" He shook
his head at the glaze of grease that held fast to the dripping
crew. "That will have to do. Follow me."

The pirates stepped one by one over the threshold and into
the outfitting room, the captain ushering his charges through to
take up the rear.

"Best get used to it, mate," he muttered to Vince, tucking a traumatized worm back behind his ear as the door closed behind them. "Followers, now. That's what we be."

"Missy, please. Stay with us, won't you?" As her son and husband cleared the table from supper, Anneke Stewart studied the small girl who sat lacing her boots on the dirt floor of the breezeway. "You can have Aunt Jean's room and you can come and go as you like…"

Missy hopped up to stand in front of Eric's mother.

"Oh, missus, I've got my hammock on-ship." Missy peered through her hair at Anneke's kind face. "If I'm not there to douse the bolts with leech oil every dawn they'll get stiff…"

Eric's mother reached out instinctively to tuck the girl's hair behind her ear and Missy startled and turned pink, looking at her feet.

"It's all stink and splinters but the Barrow's my home," she shuffled nervously. "Till they get back, I'm on watch."

"We'll set a plate for your breakfast, then." Anneke met the girl's upturned face with concerned kindness. "Take some gingerbread in case you get hungry later."

She held out a cinnamon-scented bundle and the girl reached out to clutch it to her chest.

"Th-th-thank you, ma'am." Missy backed away from the glow of the porch, her footfall light as she darted through the yard and over the hill towards her home.

"That can't be right. Nine to twelve months?"

The usual gathering of petitioners assembled at the Stewarts' kitchen table to navigate an endless bureaucracy. Having been deemed insiders given their intimate history with the crew and their exposure to its parent organization, Joe and the Stewart family were given permission to access the union's inner sanctum in a way ordinary folk had never done. The fair's indiscretions and widespread public exposure had caused thousands to witness what would usually be a closed disciplinary event—and so the veil of secrecy, thanks to the Dreads, was now irrevocably lifted.

"Nine to twelve months for the Appeals Committee to convene and review the case…after which they will decide whether or not the case is valid…upon which time they may or may not proceed with an appeals trial, which may or may not be scheduled within the twelve months following approval…"

"All that and they might just tell us to stuff it," Eric snapped.

"They might, but we've got to start somewhere," his father sighed.

"But at this rate, it's going to be months, years even! There's got to be something else we can do."

Missy was sullen as she watched the exchange. *There's the one thing I don't mind about bein' a bit different. All I got to do for peace and quiet is to turn away and quit readin' lips.* Frustration turned to heated debate and she shimmied off the bench, her woollen socks padding soundlessly on the planks of the floor.

She pressed the palm of one hand against the window that faced Joe's land, the resting place of the great wooden hulk, and felt the ship's call through the night-cooled glass.

There is *something else we can do.*

"Look at us." Amos scowled into his reflection, his menace clipped by a standard-issue hairnet, white collared shirt, and creased polyester slacks. "We's ridiculous."

Willie cocked his head to the side contemplatively.

"*Mais oui*, I'm startin' to like dese slippers."

(It was rule at union headquarters: the boots of all sentence-servers, delinquents, and duty-dodgers were confiscated in favour of crocheted multi-coloured footsies that demoralized most pirates so thoroughly they wouldn't bother trying to run even if they could.)

Amos shook his head in disgust.

"I like ma tootsies warm," Willie shrugged.

"Yer done for, yeh git. You jus' said *tootsies*. Even Frankie wouldn't say dat…"

As the two bickered in hushed tones, Vince, the once-proud first mate, shuffled by with an armful of three-ring binders bound for the photocopy room. He glared censoriously as he passed the brute and the huckster, who had gone silent, gaping after him.

"Eh *toi!*" Will called out as Vince shuffled down the hall away from them. "'Ow come you gots polka dot on yer slipper and all we gots is plain?"

Amos snorted and the first mate stopped in his tracks, turning his head just enough to growl over his shoulder.

"Not. One. Word."

Mais c'est VRAI... Will mouthed indignantly as Vince stormed away.

INTERNATIONAL TREASURE HUNTERS & USEFUL GOODS SALVAGERS SOCIETY (T.H.U.G.S.S.) HELPFUL HINTS FOR HOUSETOIL

- DO remain stationed at assigned cubicle
- DO NOT tamper with union property such as fluorescent light fixtures, sealed windows, and security cameras
- DO submit paperwork, send faxes, operate the photocopier, type reports, and format memos in a timely, gentle fashion
- DO NOT resort to physical forms of expression with union property such as computer keyboards, fax machines, and telephones
- DO restrict conversation except during designated break periods of 9:45–10:00 a.m. and 2:45-3:00 p.m. daily
- DO restrict sanctioned conversation to a volume of less than 50 decibels
- DO NOT leave the facility building except in the performance of depot platform duty
- DO visit the scrubroom at least bi-weekly in consideration for neighbouring administrators

- DO NOT attempt to invent on the premises
- DO NOT request early release

FAILURE TO COMPLY WILL RESULT IN THE IN-
TRIPLICATE ADDITION OF FAILURE-TO-COMPLY
REPORT #24-FTC TO PERSONAL FILE, AS WELL AS
SENTENCE REASSESSMENT.
THANK YOU.
ENJOY YOUR WORK TERM.

"Bernie Two Tricks, Blitzrider Trackist."

The pirate-girl was a scrawny thing in overalls, with a miner's headlamp fixed around a head of wildly frizzled hair. She was pale as a sheet and tiny by thug measure, but bumped a sure and wiry fist against that of each crewmember in turn as though she were twelve feet tall. It was morning break and so a mixed bag of pirates from all over huddled by a fence in the fog, gulping in as much fresh air as they could before the buzzer rang.

"What're you doin' here?" Johnnie asked. "Blitzers are Londoners!"

"Me da's a welder wiv da Meaner Submariners, an' I was wiv 'im fer a metalworks apprenticin', an' they got stuck in an abyss off Sable Island trawlin' for wreck scrap. Dey went fer drydock an' I was sent 'ere ter catch a ride wiv da Helians back to England but nobody seen 'em fer months, so I'm workin' instead o' waitin'..."

"Trains, right? Underground?" Phezzie was fascinated. "Mus' be a whole lotta metalwork."

"Yeh. Whole tube lines got all blowed up back in the war, an' so dey jus' brick it all up and figger it's nuffin' fer nobody. But we gots in, an' the bones was good, so we fixed up trains, propped up th' tubes. We takes our trainships an' climb upground through storm vents an' runoff pipes, take what we want, bring it back down fer transport…crikey, da time! I'm late fer th' combine drop."

As quickly as she'd popped into their circle the girl saluted briskly and skipped off.

"My goodness," marvelled Frankie as she disappeared around a corner. "We knows well 'nuff there's lots out there but it's mighty grand to meet our union brothers and sisters from away."

The others were so much in agreement that Frankie's utterance of *mighty grand* went unmocked. Then, the tallest pirate they'd ever seen—taller even than Golden—ambled towards them dressed in flannel coveralls of red-and-black plaid, as much grizzly bear as human for all his coarseness.

"Ripsaw Mick w' the Crummies up north. Who's captain here?"

Hector stepped forward and the bear-man reached out to grasp his hand firmly, meeting his eye, and in doing so made the silent claim of peer.

"The Crummies? You's the ones what scrapped a whole paper mill in one night, eh?" Meena was awestruck. "We heard o' you…"

"Sure did," his hands gestured broadly, re-enacting in the air. "See, my crew's got twenty and four crummies—dat's a one-ton truck wit' the back chopped off, and then welded onto it a flatbed, or a hydraulic lift, or d'backs of ol' schoolbuses fer quarters. We get our pickins' from treeplantin' camps, fishin' lodges, factory towns. We can carry anythin', anywhere wif' our crummies. Kin to your Barrow, I'm told, how our convoy busts t'rough woods an' bogs. We's the best choppers anywheres."

Johnnie Golden, the best chopper anywhere, sniffed derisively. Meena beamed with admiration, and Mick winked.

"Where's yer sentence slacks?" Zeke asked, tugging fitfully at his own.

The northern captain paused, glancing at the Dreads with a sudden sheepishness.

"Almost done," he shuffled from one foot to the other. "Been here six months fer evadin' paperwork. On my way back to Fort MacKenzie as soon as the confiscators bring out me crummy, and as soon as I can get 'er runnin' again. May be a few days out, yet, but I'll be off the bad books. How long fer you lot?"

"Longer than that," Hector sighed as the buzzer called them back to the beige. "Longer than that."

Chapter Fifteen

THE BRIGHT SIDE OF DISOBEDIENCE

Joe enjoyed the untroubled sleep of an ethical, hard-working man. And a good thing it was, too, for the nervy souls who tiptoed away from his cot just before midnight did so without a hint of alarm.

The note was tied with twine around the old man's thumb.

DEAR JOE.
Me and Missy are going to get the Dreads.
Taking the ship. We'll go slow mostly. Missy's been teaching me ropes and cogs.
See you soon. Bye.

Eric

"That way," Missy pointed. Eric swept the flashlight over the crinkled surface of Meena's geological chart, traced the route with his finger, and nodded in agreement. "We oughta stay clear of roads as long as we can…"

"We can follow the power lines along the edge of these crown woods, then at the quarry we can cut back onto the old road through Lunenburg," he whispered. "We need to make Halifax before dawn, 'cause we'll have to go straight down Barrington Street to get to the industrial park and we don't want to get stuck in morning traffic…"

He looked up from the map to find her eyes locked keenly on him. In recent weeks he'd become accustomed to how intently she observed his face—and everything around her, for that matter—for this was how she made up her mind about things, more through sight than sound.

"A rollin' kickstart, then, and let's hope Joe sleeps through the shake of it," she winked and a brave recklessness passed between them. "You winch the landlines. I'll crank the pistons, then once I let off the brake, pop the clutch."

"Got it." Eric swung round to grasp the winch handle, knocking the clutch into place with his foot as he freed the ship from its leashes.

Good thing he's not one of those indoor boys. In the still velvet midnight Missy shivered and bent to the pistons, beaming from behind her hair.

The Barrow had never tiptoed before but on this night, it crept to the rescue at a near-neutral roll. Not only were the two shipmates of a much smaller stature than the brutes for whom the ship was built, but this night was their one chance to disobey, to rebel—and they could not afford the melee of a scene, for chances like that are never granted twice. The ship eased away from Joe's cabin at midnight, and at one o'clock in the morning she passed silently through the village of Barss Corner, past the merchant, the tackle shop, the bakery. By three-thirty the darkness had thinned a little as the Barrow gently rolled down Lunenburg's Montague Street. The famed schooner *Bluenose II*, tucked into the berth of her home port, had been enjoying her slumber but one ship always senses another, and from the ribs of her bow to the tip of her mast the tall sailing ship stirred with knowing, urging her land-borne cousin on to glory.

Missy admired the lines of the schooner from the helm and felt the kinship of the fastest tall ship that ever was, noted its approving nod. *Our Barrow, she's got respect now, and havin' is gettin'.*

The screen door banged behind him as Joe burst into the Stewarts' kitchen.

"Joe!" Eric's father startled in mid-pour, and he raised the coffee pot in a gesture of welcome. "Care for a mug?"

"Can't…have to hurry…the kids…" Joe panted, just having sprinted over the hill.

"Not a peep from either of 'em. How's that happen, anyways? One minute they're ten and the next minute they're teenagers that sleep in past chores. Busy day yesterday, though, Eric was helping Missy with something on the Barrow..."

Joe shook his head and at the expression on his face, Anneke Stewart raised her hand to her chest.

"They've...gone. They've taken the ship...gone to the city, to try and...lord, who knows. They think they'll be able to get the pirates out."

Before Joe had finished speaking, breakfast had been abandoned and boots were already on, hands fumbling for keys.

"To the truck." Eric's father was already on the outside steps. "We'll take the highway. We might catch up."

Lothar Lothario, Greaser with the Meaner Submariners, sat inside the warehouse on the receiving dock with his chair tipped back and his feet up, his hat over his face. It wasn't yet dawn, after all, and no drops were scheduled for this night shift.

Dive!

His foot twitched, immersed in a dream so real he could almost smell the diesel.

Shut the hatches! Dive, boys, dive!

The fumes in his nostrils were so vivid they charged him to run from rules and rice cakes and fluorescent lights, to storm and froth as was his nature's will.

PSST.

A finger poked his shoulder.

PIRATE.

Then again, a poke—this time more of a slight shove. He grunted and swatted it away.

SHIP REPORTING FOR PICKUP.

With a yelp the pirate tilted backwards, crashing to the floor and then leaping up to his feet in a single motion.

"Siryessir all's good...wha?"

He rubbed his eyes and looked up, and up, then down again.

"A'int no such thing as pickup. Drops, only drops..." he murmured.

Two children stood before him—children!—with hands on their hips and sneak on their faces. At their backs was the thing that had called to him in his sleep—the grandest, wildest, most smashing landship of all, its hull littered with the bites and bruises of a lifetime of thunderous crashing.

"That's... that's...THE BARROW!" he sputtered. "How'd you get past the checkpoints? The sensors? The cameras? Impossible..."

He looked beyond them and saw the massive freight doors had been opened from the outside, as well as three padlocked gates in his line of sight, the last in a series of over a dozen. The girl, a feisty-looking scamp, stepped forward with a nerve he'd never seen before in ordinary folk, let alone little ones.

"We near about bumped yer nose when we pulled in here, you dozin' like a baby," she craned to see around him for signs of a raised alarm. "Sensors are there for ships what rumble."

"We don't rumble," the boy added.

Lothar's jaw opened and snapped shut again, agog.

"No time to 'splain," the girl hissed. "Listen. Yer Johnnie's, right? Johnnie Golden's cousin?"

He nodded.

"Go get 'em for us. Go get the Dreads an' tell 'em Missy's 'ere for 'em..." She paused and turned to look at the boy, who stood firm beside her. "...And the tracker kid too. It's a bustin' out."

He raised one finger in the air in a gesture of waiting.

"Night-desk, come in night-desk," he spoke calmly into his walkie-talkie, not taking his eyes from the girl and the boy. A voice replied.

"This is the night-desk. Go ahead, depot."

"All's quiet down 'ere. No drops fer another couple hours. I need me a break fer th' crapper."

The voice on the other end of the radio sighed disapprovingly.

"Mate, you are at headquarters, not on ship. Please use office-appropriate language when referring to the toilet."

"Yes, sir. Sorry, sir." He rolled his eyes and the boy grinned.

"You may go. Two minutes."

"Thank you, sir. Back in a jiff."

He clipped the radio back onto his belt and motioned to this Missy and the boy she called Tracker.

"You two get back on board." The ship puttered softly as its pilots mounted the chain net. "Gimme two minutes. Start countin' soon as I close that door. Get to zero an' GO—those Dreads'll find their way on board. Two minutes. If yer not movin', they'll catch us all."

He slipped through the doorway that led to the dormitory but before shutting the door behind him, he popped his head through the crack.

"Y'know what's enough to make a washed-up old brute like me feel wicked again?" He grinned. "Disobedience."

He offered a fist and Missy bumped it with hers, and then he did the same with Eric, who hesitated but gave his fist a shy knock in return.

"Good lad," he nodded in encouragement, sensing that the girl was kin but the boy was not. Then he was gone.

Eric looked at his watch.

One minute, fifteen seconds

He tapped nervously on the indicator glass of the engine block. It was in-gear and humming.

One minute, five seconds

He checked the crankshaft for grease as Missy had shown him. It was still slick despite the nightlong journey.

Fifty-five seconds

He had already released the clutch chain but loosened it again, just to be sure.

Forty-five seconds

Missy was in the hold, her being more versed with the

throwing of ropes. The yawning chasm at the stern would allow the crew to leap aboard straight from the platform without the steep climb to the topdeck, which left Eric high above at the helm—at least until Missy or the pirates appeared to take over.

Fifteen seconds

"Pump the pistons!" Missy's voice called from below. Eric gulped. One, two, three, four. It was done.

Ten seconds

"Pop the handbrake!"

Eric grasped the lever with both hands and pulled.

"It's jammed!" he cried fruitlessly, as Missy was not in range of sight or sound.

Two seconds

"NOW!" Missy's voice cried. He raised his feet off the ground, throwing all his weight on the lever, but the brake wouldn't budge.

"TRACKER! STEP ON IT!" Missy shrieked.

From through the closed doors Eric heard a stampede and beyond that, voices raised in alarm. He put both feet against the brakebox and pushed with his legs while pulling with his arms.

"ERIC!" she screamed. "THEY'RE COMING!"

"GRAAAAAAGH!" he grunted, and the lever came unstuck, pitching him hard onto the deck. The door burst open and through it came a tangle of roaring polyester pirates, knocking into each other and sliding across the concrete floor in…knitted slippers? He scrambled to his feet and pounced upon the accelerator with one hand, gripping the wheel with the other, white-knuckled and shaking.

Just like driving a tractor just like driving a tractor just like driving a tractor...

"AIAIAIAIAIAIAAEEEEE!" Missy's triumphant call was answered by a chorus of roughworn voices as a writhing mass of pirates made for the open hold.

In running leaps they hurled themselves off the end of the platform, limbs flying. The first few made it—some Missy didn't recognize—and landed with a series of crashes, rolling violently across the hold before finding their feet. Ewsula near-flattened Missy and Willie overshot his jump, careening across the decking and out a drainage hole on the other side, clinging by his fingertips to the hull until he was pulled back inside by Zeke. The ship was well clear of the platform now, and it lurched as Eric turned the wheel to steer towards the gigantic bay doors.

"ROPES!" Missy cried, tossing an array of anchored lines to those attempting running leaps and to those still entangled in the doorway's bottleneck. Ike, Amos, Meena, and three more hangers-on landed in almost simultaneous two-footed thumps, the wooden planks quaking beneath them, and Frankie climbed hand-over-hand up a line thrown and held by Johnnie. Having missed the chance to leap aboard, Phezzie and an acrobatic, wiry pirate girl had both scurried up the network of pipes that ran along the walls and ceiling, and after swinging from one to the other like on monkey bars they both let go to crash onto the top deck.

"Right good steerin', kid!" Phezzie yelled above the confusion. "I'll wind the motordrive for some speed, we's are gonna need it..."

"OI! Gimme somefin' teh do!" the girl yelled. Eric surrendered the clutch and she grasped it without hesitating and shrieked, her face flushed with thrill. "CHUUUUFFF! BLITZERS ON DECK!"

From the platform Vince swung Sam round like a shotput, launching him close enough to catch the outstretched hand of a bearlike giant in black-and-red plaid who swung wildly from the chain net. Reggie and Gretchen catapulted themselves from a high stack of crates, the arc of the coxswain's leap bringing her head within an inch of the top edge of the hold door.

"HALT!" an amplified voice rang out from within the bowels of the building and a familiar siren whined long and loud.

"CAPTAIN!" Missy leaned off the farthest edge of the hold as the ship pulled away, one hand cupping her mouth. "VINCE!"

The crew gawked at one another for a hurried inventory— curiously they'd attracted more bodies than the ship commanded (for no matter their origin all pirates shared the trait of opportunism, and none relished paperwork). But they were missing two of their own.

"RUN!"

The pirates all bellowed at once as the depot's bay doors began to close, a rapidly narrowing exit between the just-escaped Barrow and the inside of the warehouse. The captain and his first mate, compelled by their stations, had stayed on the platform flinging and shoving and urging as many pirates as they could to the refuge of the ship, and in doing so had missed their own chances.

"RUUUUN!"

Just as a team of officers burst through the dormitory door, the two pirates leapt in unison off the platform and onto the asphalt, sprinting across the warehouse floor with creased slacks flapping at their ankles.

They squeezed through the last sliver of open door before it shut with a clang and the Barrow, safely outside, erupted in victorious whoops. The captain and his first mate leapt into the hold and were thoroughly tackled by the exhilarated crew. The wooden hulk then weaved back through the maze of gates as the sun rose over Halifax Harbour, illuminating open roads as well as the notorious ship in all its glory.

Just like that, the Barrow and its crew (and then some) were gone. The union officers left on the platform gaped at one another in shock.

"You see what I saw?" one Red said to the other. "First-ever stealth approach. Gets past every checkpoint, every camera, every sensor—straight through the city, for that matter—then makes off clean with a whole crew."

"None of us even came out of the staff room till we heard the brutes yelling," added a second. "That ship...that ship was a ghost."

"Good thing it's the end of the night shift. I wouldn't want to answer to Chief this morning," a third shuddered.

There was a long silence as the Barrow's feat reverberated through the warehouse. Then an old red flatbed truck approached, circling once and then again before edging tentatively through the reopened bay doors.

A friendly looking man leaned out the window, two more faces peering around him from inside the cab.

"Lovely morning, yes?" the man's voice was oddly strained. The officers blinked, unaccustomed to passersby—especially at six o'clock in the morning.

"Just wondering... any of you folks seen ahhh...a very large, wooden..."

"That way," a junior officer shouted, pointing back towards the city.

"Excellent. D'you happen to know, were there two..."

"...Two kids? Sure was," the officer continued, so indelibly impressed he forgot himself and his uniform entirely. "Saw one of 'em piloting the thing all by himself!"

The driver and his passengers embraced and cried out happily.

"Pardon me again, but did they have with them any p—"

"Pirates? The whole lot. Gone."

"Crackerjack! Thank you so much." The man smiled broadly as did his passengers, a woman and a spritely old man. "So much, thank you!"

The red truck turned and puttered back towards the gate, hands waving out each window. As it turned onto the road towards downtown, a jubilant call was thrown out onto the wind.

AAAAIAIAIAIAIAAEEE!!

"Best clock out while we can, folks..."

As slick as hooligans the officers scattered, none inclined to explain their failure to give chase. For in the face of the Barrow's unlawful flight it was undeniable: this morning's dawn had brought with it the most radical pirate manoeuvring ever witnessed.

Dear Ms. Chief,

The letter was written in immaculate penmanship on a crisp, upstanding paper that carried with it the wholesome scents of woodsmoke and cinnamon.

It has been many months now since the capture and escape of the Dread Crew. I write to you today with solidarity, for like you, I know how difficult it is to be cast in the role of pirate shepherd. I cannot abide the unseemly wasting of energy, not to mention

*finding rat tails in the bottom of my tea. I believe in consideration
and economy of movement, neither of which align too well with
unplanned explosions. What tends to be scoffed at by pirates is held in
the greatest regard by the both of us, I think—order, and reliability,
and, naturally, favourable profit margins.*

*Please find enclosed letters of appeal written by citizens on the
Dread Crew's behalf, petitioning their readiness—and indeed
their enthusiasm—to cooperate with the enterprise of collecting
and refurbishing junk without the unsavoury tactics once deemed
necessary. We humbly request that you rescind all housetoil
warrants and declare the crew free to come and go as they please in
your name.*

*They say you catch more flies with honey than with vinegar.
I used to suspect the truth of it but now, thanks to the Dreads, I
know it. Their citizen friends have remitted junk on their behalf to
the tune of multiple drops per quarter—verified as Dread-earned
by signed affidavit—in order to ensure their continued release
but also their good standing. I do hope that all these drops have
counted on your books as legitimate, and measured towards their
performance, for it is their own work, and we are only the mode of
delivery. I thank you for your willingness to accept what represents
a job well done.*

Yours in Union Brotherhood,
Signed Grampa "The Jackal" Joe
Witnessed by Eric "The Tracker" Stewart
Honourary T.H.U.G.G. Brothers Local 262

The chief of all chiefs turned the letter over in her hands, placing it on her desk and smoothing its folds absently. She sighed as her eyes fell upon the other stack of paper on her desk—a memo tacked to the front of a file folder marked DREAD CREW (BARROW—MARITIME REGION).

INVENTORY/ASSETS
PERFORMANCE REVIEW
FALL/WINTER

CAPTAIN, Dread Crew
Maritime Region, Canada
+ minor forays into Northeastern New England
(Barrow Wood Ship* [1]; Gooperator Offensive Cannon** [1];
Junk 'n' Joy Citizens Festival*** [annual])

* refurbished for stealth
** refurbished for public relations value
*** public outreach exercise

JUNK SALVAGING & DEPOT DROPS
PERCENTAGE -UNDER/+OVER QUOTA

May	NIL
June	NIL

July   NIL
August   + 118%
September + 136%
October   + 165% [1]
November + 180% [2]
December   + 214% [3]

(1) all-time record
(2) all-time record
(3) all-time record

In the privacy of her office she muttered aloud to herself, as she always did.

Numbers don't lie.

She thumbed the folder's contents—complaints and advisories and disciplinary actions and quota reports, all stamped DELINQUENT. With one tentative finger she nudged the folder to the edge of her desk, then a little farther.

"Hup!" she exclaimed as it flopped into the recycle bin below, noting for the first time in her life the unusual but refreshing rush of impulsiveness.

Countless decades of thuggery failed to match the triumph of the Barrow's return to junk-hunting. The pirates' eventual pardon, published in the classifieds section of the newspaper under "miscellaneous," spread like wildfire and inspired friendly honks and open doors from gentle folk at every destination.

Citizens from all over flocked to Barrow appearances in one town or the next, grateful to do right by construction debris and spring cleanings and industrial leftovers. Every stop inspired scrap swaps and brainstorms, the crew deluged to the point of frantic with an unheard-of bounty, with so much junk and so many new junk-inclined friends they could hardly keep up.

From an upstairs window, Eric spotted an unmistakable column of smoke approaching from the distant west.

She's back. She's really back.

He yanked a fleece over his head as he tumbled down the stairs, reaching for his tools on his way out the back door. By the time the ship had finally whooshed to a halt in the yard, a small crowd of neighbours had gathered. The pirates hollered greetings and Eric leapt forward to catch the first landline, driving a cleat firmly into the earth with his heel and anchoring the rope in one swift flick. He stood up, smiling, hands on his hips. Missy swung down the zip-pole looking wilder and filthier than ever but beaming like sunshine on water.

He's no indoor boy.

Joe and the captain leaned against the Stewarts' peacock shed as the crew hosed down the muddy Barrow, gruff and merry voices echoing through the dusk. It was well into fall now, and the pirates had returned with brutes aplenty to help prune the bramble for next year's blackberry crop. Later that night Eric's mother and father would outdo themselves, collaborating with Zeke on the most epic feast ever seen, the first of many.

"Here, Hector." Joe passed the weathered, dreadlocked giant a cherry tomato fresh off the vine. "Brought somethin' for you from my garden."

The captain's filthy finger and thumb pinched the humble roundness from Joe's outstretched palm and examined it doubtfully.

"Measly thing…won't hold a candle to a cold beetle sup, I'd bet."

He popped it into his mouth, shut his jaw, and startled as the treat burst sweet in his cheeks.

"Candy, that is," he leaned forward for more. "To think I'd never have done anythin' with that teensy nub aside get it stuck in the grooves of a boot!"

The brutes were already waist-deep in the bramble, yowching at the thorns and shouting barbs at one another. The sound of a muffled explosion, then a furious roar, emitted from the galley and a gang of goats harrumphed through the field bleating indignantly. With the help of Reggie and Sam, Eric's parents stoked a glorious bonfire that shot sparks high into the sky. The sight and smell of it spread through the hills, and neighbours strolled up the lane bearing food and good cheer. Frankie and Amos emerged from the farmhouse lugging armfuls of white fabric and the old film projector under the direction of Missy, all of them brimming with fascination.

An old man I am…

Joe offered the pint of tomatoes to the pirate captain, who grinned, a dribble of seedy juice escaping out the corner of his mouth.

...but here I've got this brand new set of eyeballs, and that makes nothin' the same, never again, and isn't it grand.

CLICK.

The boy came out from around the corner of the shed and lowered the old Polaroid camera from his face, looking from Joe to Hector and back again.

"Gotcha," Eric grinned.

Epilogue

Transformed from VAGABOND OUTLAWS to respected REJIGGERS and ADVENTURERS EXTRAORDINAIRE, the Dread Crew has ventured farther than ever before by way of abandoned logging roads and railway lines, their reputation preceding them in a most welcome and profitable manner.

Captain HECTOR GRISTLE remains chief-in-command of the Dreads, orbiting the crew's adventures around the centrepoint of Joe's land. The Dreads rumble back to Joe's homestead every few weeks to raid his tomato patch, soak in the pond, and rest weary feet in exchange for news and trinkets.

First Mate Vincent the VILE remains second-in-command of the Dreads, supplementing his duties with a newfound entrepreneurial venture. When the ship rolls into a large enough town, he sells out Dread Head Moshpits, marshalling the crew to teach locals about the vigour to be had by way of a well-timed jig. Navigator SCREEMIN' Meena, in addition to route-finding, serves as MC and band leader on such occasions.

Coxswain FETCHIN' Gretchen and Brute Ewsula THE
BARBARIAN continue on as Barrow crew, with occasional
sabbaticals among gentle folk who hire them out for their
barbequing and maze-building expertise.

Machinist FUNKY Phezekiah invented a Portable Lemon
and Rock Salt Shower—the Scrubbin' Lemon-Aider. When he
eats seaweed, onion, and Limburger sandwiches it shrieks and
the powerwash arm springs from his hat and douses him (and
anyone else in close proximity), solving the stink but causing
quite another ruckus altogether.

Huckster ILL Willie Cusson, Logdriver Johnnie
GOLDEN, and Slopjack Zeke THE GREEK Popadopoulos
remain at their Barrow posts—combusting, cursing, and
cooking respectively.

Jury-Rigger WEDGIE Reggie has become a popular
stand-up comedian, a pirate by day and performer by night,
although children are only allowed into his shows with earmuffs
on, because he is truly disgusting, and only the rudest of
townspeople find him funny.

Brute FAMOUS Amos went to Hollywood to make his
name as a character actor. He is said to be "happier than a
slug in slop" and visits the crew from time to time in order to
refresh his method and supplement Zeke's pantry with strange
American foodstuffs.

Knotjack CRANKY Frankie is thrilled to have finally earned
a permanent station on the Barrow. He took on the role vacated

by Missy (see below), his good cheer being the best and first line of diplomacy with ordinary folk.

Gunnder SLIMEBUCKET Sam continues to be in charge of the Gooperator, and is tasked with concocting blackberry sploosh around the clock. Thanks to Missy and Ike's berry tending, Sam has more sploosh than he has targets—almost.

Under the tutelage and shared interest of Missy Bullseye, Brute IRONBOUND Ike has found his words in sign language. Before a fateful encounter with an enraged razorclam on his native Digby shore, Ike had been round the world more times than Joe. His newfound language has revealed a wealth of stories almost too wild to be believed, all of which beg to be heard after so long in muteness. Missy serves as his translator and in firelight the pirates are enraptured, and forgive the both of them the private jokes they share at the expense of everyone else.

It is the aspiration of Mairi MISSY BULLSEYE to one day be mistress of her own ship, and to command her own crew. Having been noted by the Reds themselves as being quite the prodigy, she has been given a special grant for an apprenticeship with the Dreads—with sabbaticals among far-flung crews of all kinds—to study the politics, tactics, mechanics, and economy of pirate life.

Bertha MRS. KNICKERS Pringle is a celebrated source of odds and ends, her old shipyard proving a near-bottomless gold mine of junk and indispensable metal scrap. To Bertha the pirate crew brings the pleasure of like-minded company, leaving her

shanty empire a little tidier with every visit and winning favour
by building play structures and skulk-friendly caves that the
wild cats appreciate as much as their queen.

Joe the JACKAL remains on his land, serving sweet,
hot tea and whoopie pies to his neighbours and stoking the
warm welcome of his pot-bellied stove. He is the local pirate
ambassador, his homestead the famed college that awards the
mandatory MMHP designation (Master Marauder in Honey
Pirating). Tales of the Dreads' highly profitable integration into
civilized society have spread fast, and Joe is now visited by crews
from all over the world. Each of them tests his patience in one
way or another, and as he teaches them how to step more lightly
on the earth (or the ocean floor, or the mountainside, or the
cave depths) each of them teaches him a thing or two about the
virtues of a hooligan life.

Eric THE TRACKER Stewart runs the new hundred-acre
blackberry tangle that has overtaken the old family woodlot,
a brilliant compromise that allows him to keep one foot in
ordinary life (and school, and chores) and one foot in pirate
life. It is an immense task to tend the prickly but valuable crop
that feeds the insatiable Gooperator, but a critical one—for
the annual splooshing is the most popular attraction at the
Junk 'n' Joy Fair, which has grown, like the bramble, beyond all
expectations. Most notably, the once-ordinary boy relishes in
abundant proof that the world is indeed more mysterious than
the outer edges of all he knows.

As Joe says from his rocking chair, sharing with his neighbour the glow of marshmallow embers: *It's the wild wind and thunder that scrubs the sky clean and blue like sapphires. The wild and thundery wind—that's what keeps you sharp.*

Kate Inglis is a writer, photographer, and mother of two boys. This is her first novel. Kate lives on the edge of a meat-grinder sea on the far eastern coastline of Nova Scotia, where she was born.
www.kateinglis.com

For more about the Dread Crew, including notes and photographs from Eric's pirate tracking diary, a "Which Pirate Are You?" quiz, the chance to ask real pirates your questions, and much more, visit
thedreadcrew.com

The Dread Crew
ROSTER

HECTOR THE
WRECKER GRISTLE
Captain

FUNKY PHEZEKIAH
Machinist

FETCHIN GRETCHEN
Coxswain

EWSULA THE
BARBARIAN
Brute

ILL WILLIE CUSSON
Huckster

JOHNNIE GOLDEN
Logdriver